Sports Illustrated KIDS

GRAPHIC NOVELS

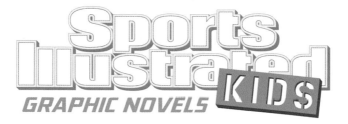

STONE ARCH BOOKS
a capstone imprint

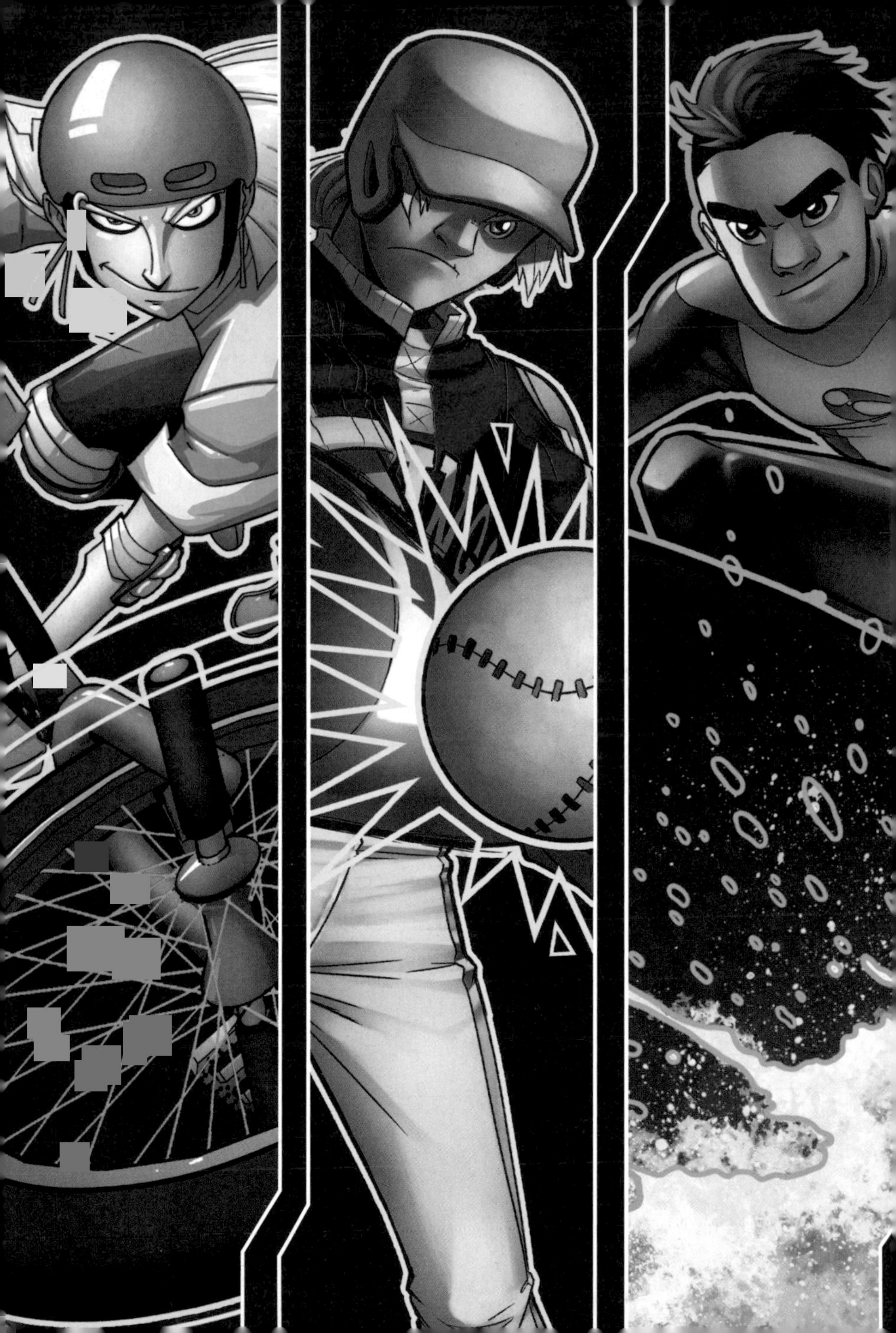

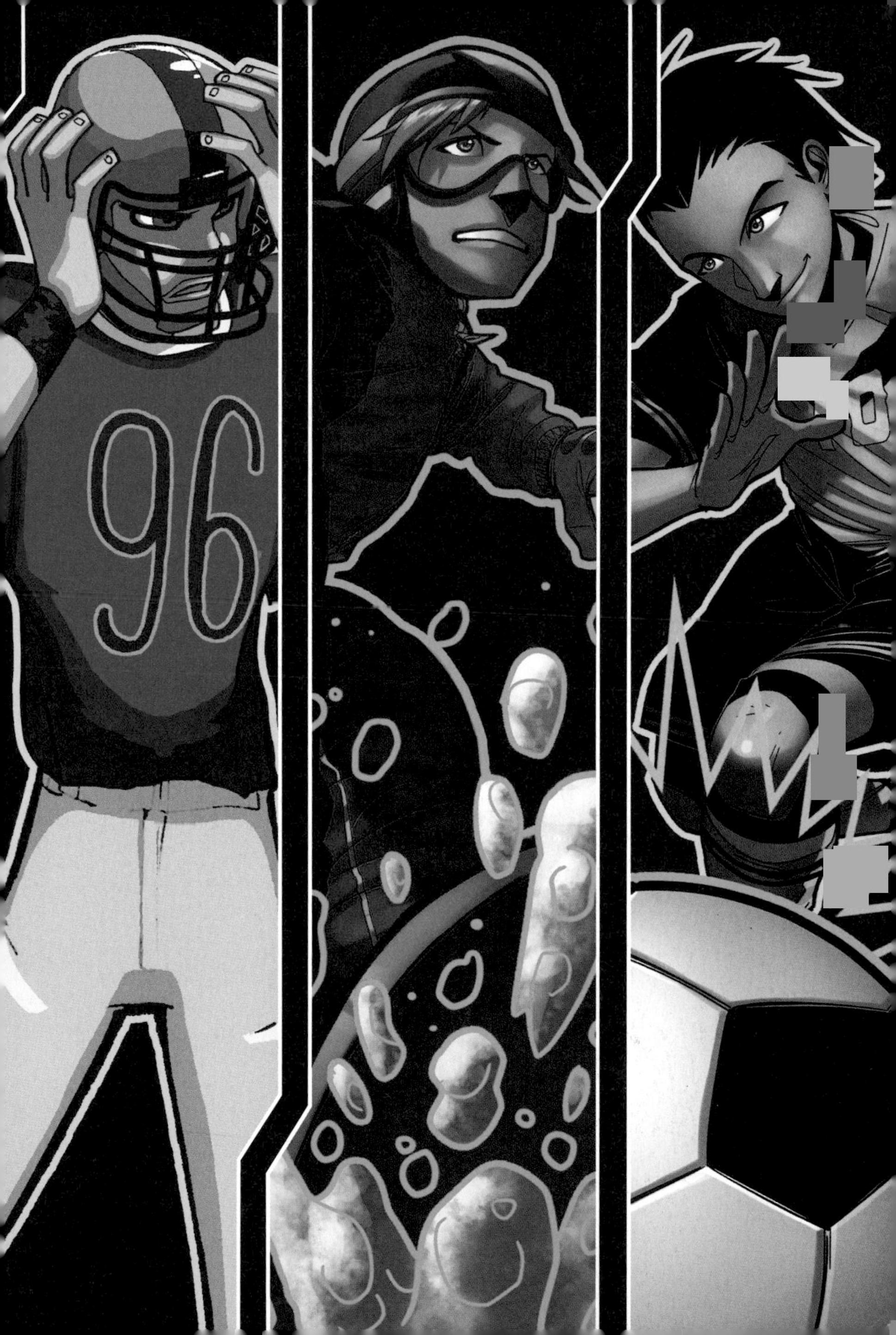

UP NEXT ›››

on Sports Illustrated KIDS

:02 SPORTS ZONE SPECIAL REPORT

:04 FEATURE PRESENTATION:

POWER AT THE PLATE

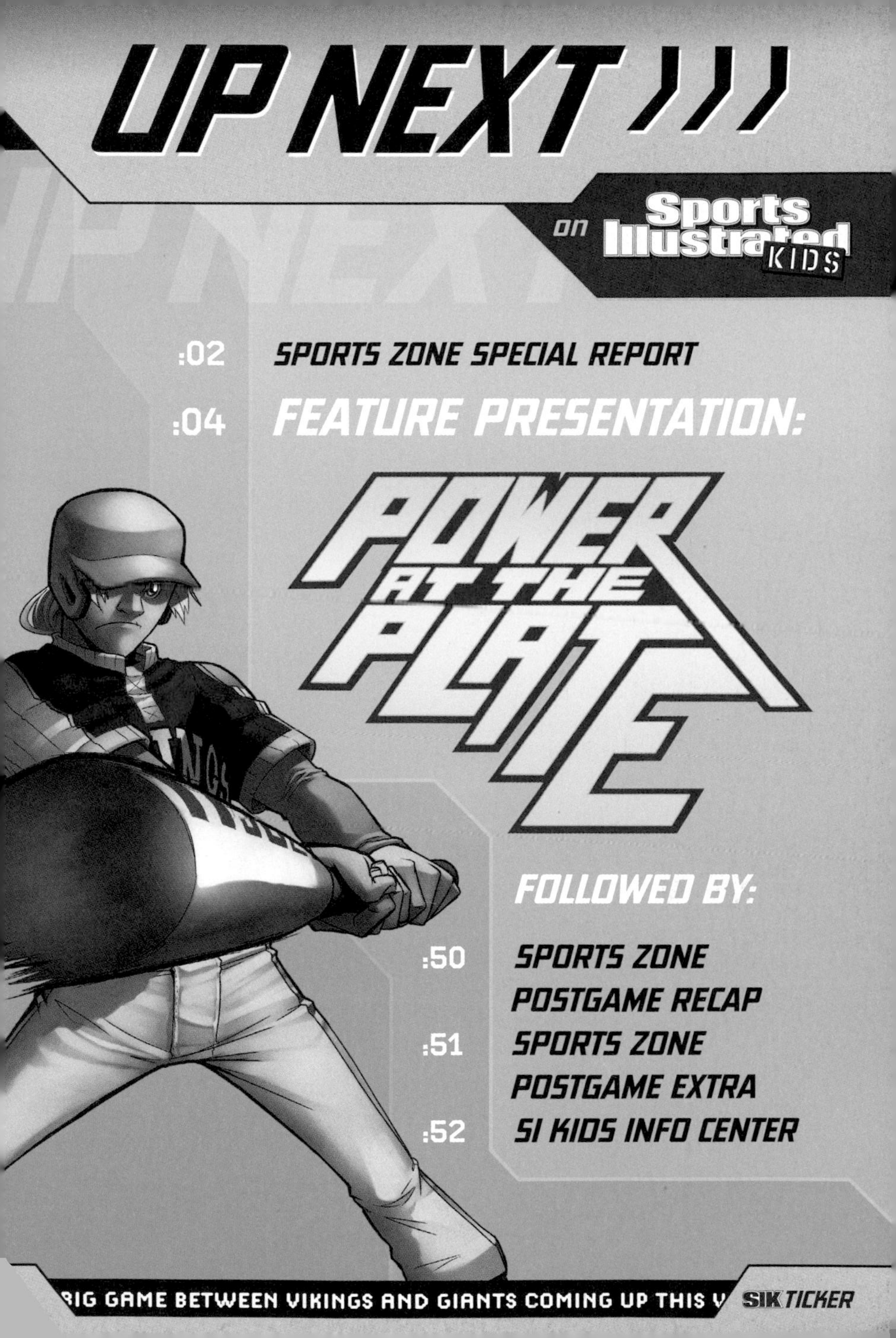

FOLLOWED BY:

:50 SPORTS ZONE POSTGAME RECAP

:51 SPORTS ZONE POSTGAME EXTRA

:52 SI KIDS INFO CENTER

BIG GAME BETWEEN VIKINGS AND GIANTS COMING UP THIS SIK TICKER

SPORTS ZONE
SPECIAL REPORT

BSL
BASEBALL

PNT
PAINTBALL

SOC
SOCCER

FBL
FOOTBALL

BBL
BASKETBALL

HKY

FEUDING STEPBROTHERS ARE HOLDING BACK THE VIKINGS

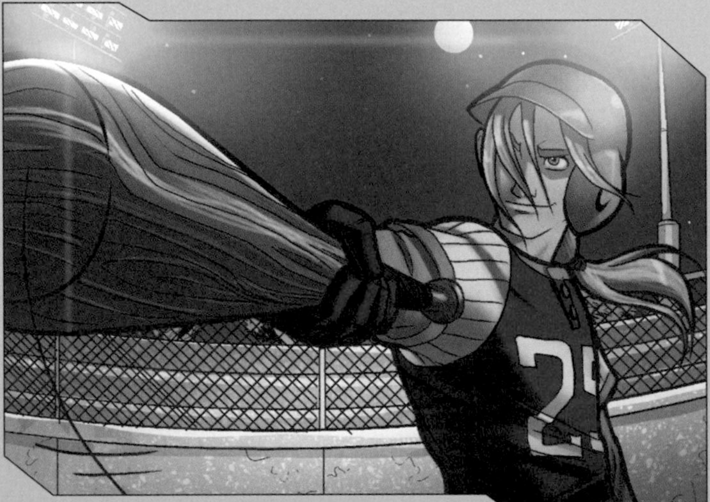

JAKE THORSON

STATS
AGE: 15
POSITION: FIRST BASE

BIO: Jake Thorson is a gifted athlete. Bigger, stronger, and faster than most everyone else his age, Jake's developed a reputation as a feared power hitter. Wielding his father's bat, Stormbreaker, Jake holds team records in home runs, runs batted in, and slugging percentage. Everyone is a fan of Jake — everyone but his stepbrother, Luke...

Sports Illustrated KIDS

UP NEXT: POWER AT THE PLATE

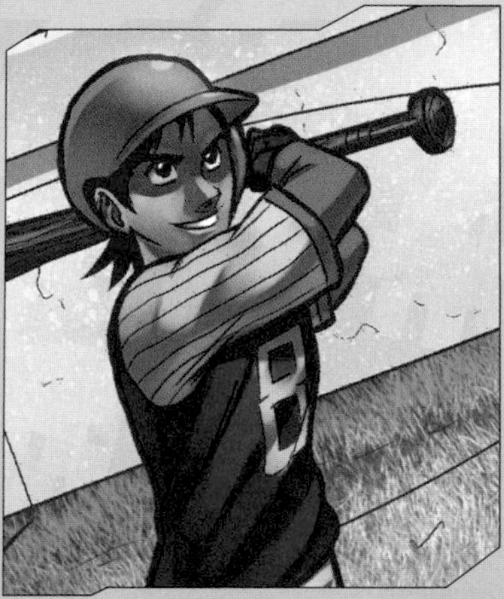

LUKE THORSON

AGE: 14

POSITION: SHORTSTOP

BIO: Luke's always felt like he got the short end of the stick. He's smaller, less athletic, and not as well-liked as his stepbrother, Jake. Their dad also gave Jake his prized baseball bat, Stormbreaker, which Luke had always wanted for himself. Nevertheless, Luke is clever — and a solid contact hitter.

BLZ vs BKS 3-1
TGR vs RDR 33-32
EAG vs BAN 14-7
SPA vs WLD 4-3
BAN vs RDR 21-15
RZR vs LIG 4-3
BLZ vs BKS 3-1

COACH ODENKIRK

AGE: 44

BIO: Coach Odenkirk runs a tight ship. He has no patience for slackers and expects all his players to act like adults and always be prepared.

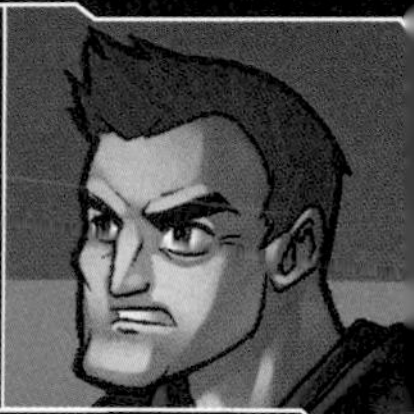

DAVE BALDI

AGE: 14

BIO: Dave is one of the Vikings' best hitters. He's friendly, quiet, and dependable.

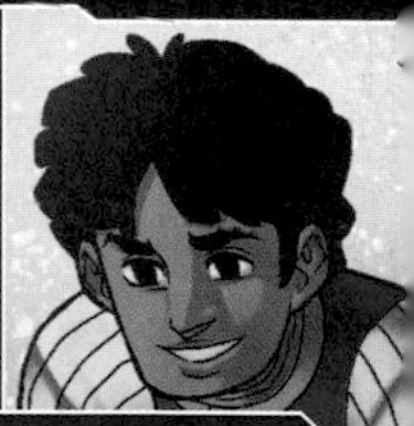

DEE DAVIS

AGE: 14

BIO: Dee is the Giants' team captain. He's also their best pitcher and hitter. He's big, mean, and has a reputation as a dirty player.

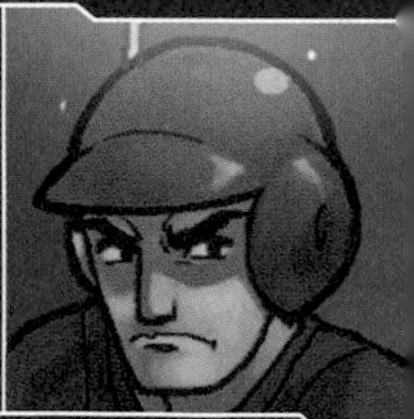

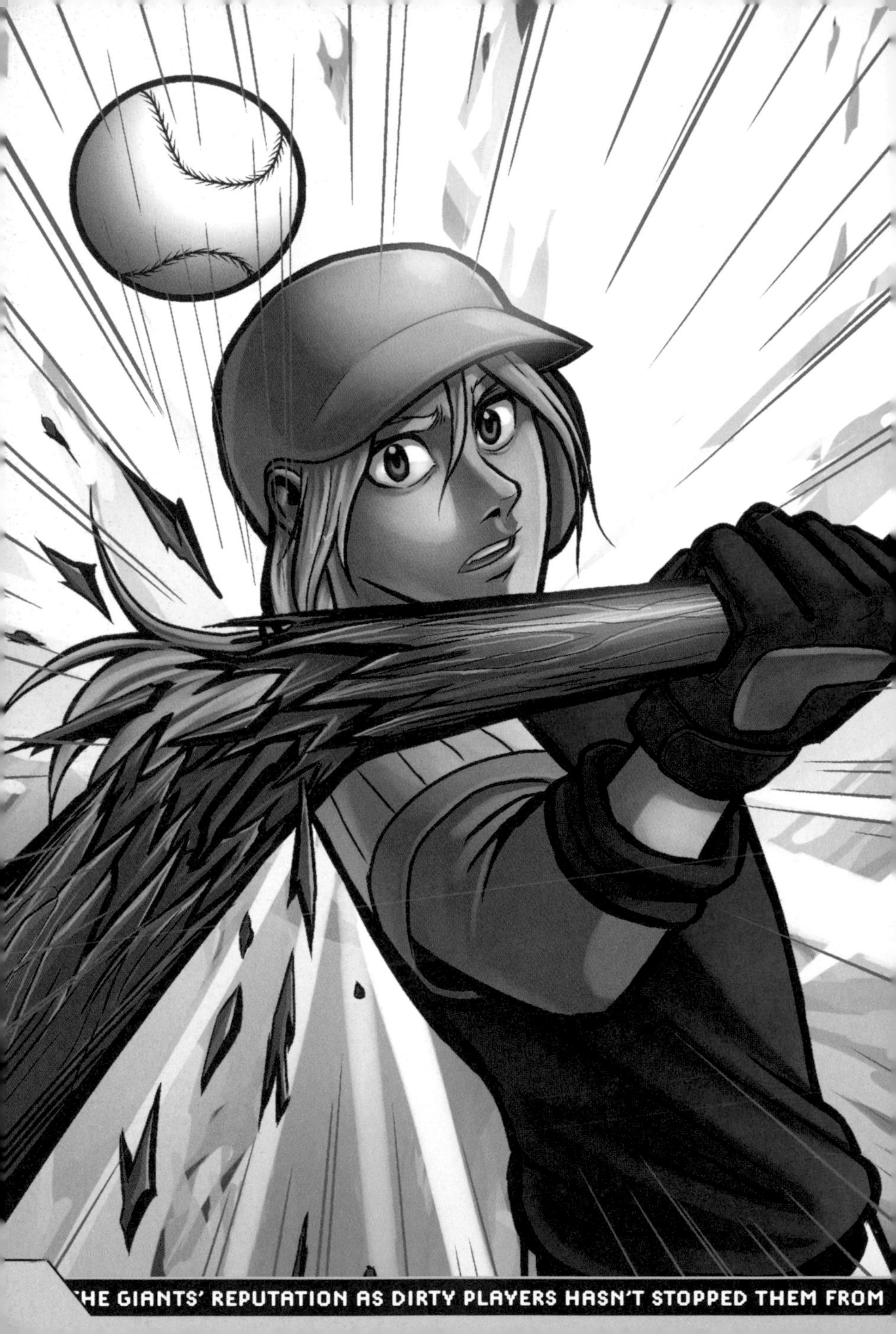
THE GIANTS' REPUTATION AS DIRTY PLAYERS HASN'T STOPPED THEM FROM

PRESENTS

A PRODUCTION OF

STONE ARCH BOOKS
a capstone imprint

written by *Scott Ciencin*
penciled by *Zoar Huerta*
inked by *Angelica Bracho*
colored by *Fernando Cano*

designed and directed by *Bob Lentz*
edited by *Sean Tulien*
creative direction by *Heather Kindseth*
editorial management by *Donald Lemke*
editorial direction by *Michael Dahl*

Sports Illustrated KIDS *Power at the Plate* is published by Stone Arch Books,
151 Good Counsel Drive, P.O. Box 669, Mankato, Minnesota 56002.
www.capstonepub.com

Copyright © 2012 by Stone Arch Books, a Capstone imprint.

All rights reserved. No part of this publication may be reproduced in whole or in
part, or stored in a retrieval system, or transmitted in any form or by any means,
electronic, mechanical, photocopying, recording, or otherwise, without written
permission of the publisher, or where applicable Time Inc.
For information regarding permissions, write to Stone Arch Books,
151 Good Counsel Drive, P.O. Box 669, Dept. R, Mankato, Minnesota 56002.
SI KIDS is a trademark of Time Inc. Used with permission.

Printed in the United States of America in Stevens Point, Wisconsin.
032011   006111WZF11

Summary: Luke Thorson isn't half as popular as his older stepbrother,
Jake, and he's had enough of hiding in his big brother's shadow ...

Cataloging-in-Publication data is available at the Library of congress
website.

ISBN 978-1-4342-2239-8 (library binding)
ISBN 978-1-4342-3400-1 (paperback)

BIG GAMES — THEY HAVE WON ELEVEN STRAIGHT AND THEY COU

SIK*TICKER*

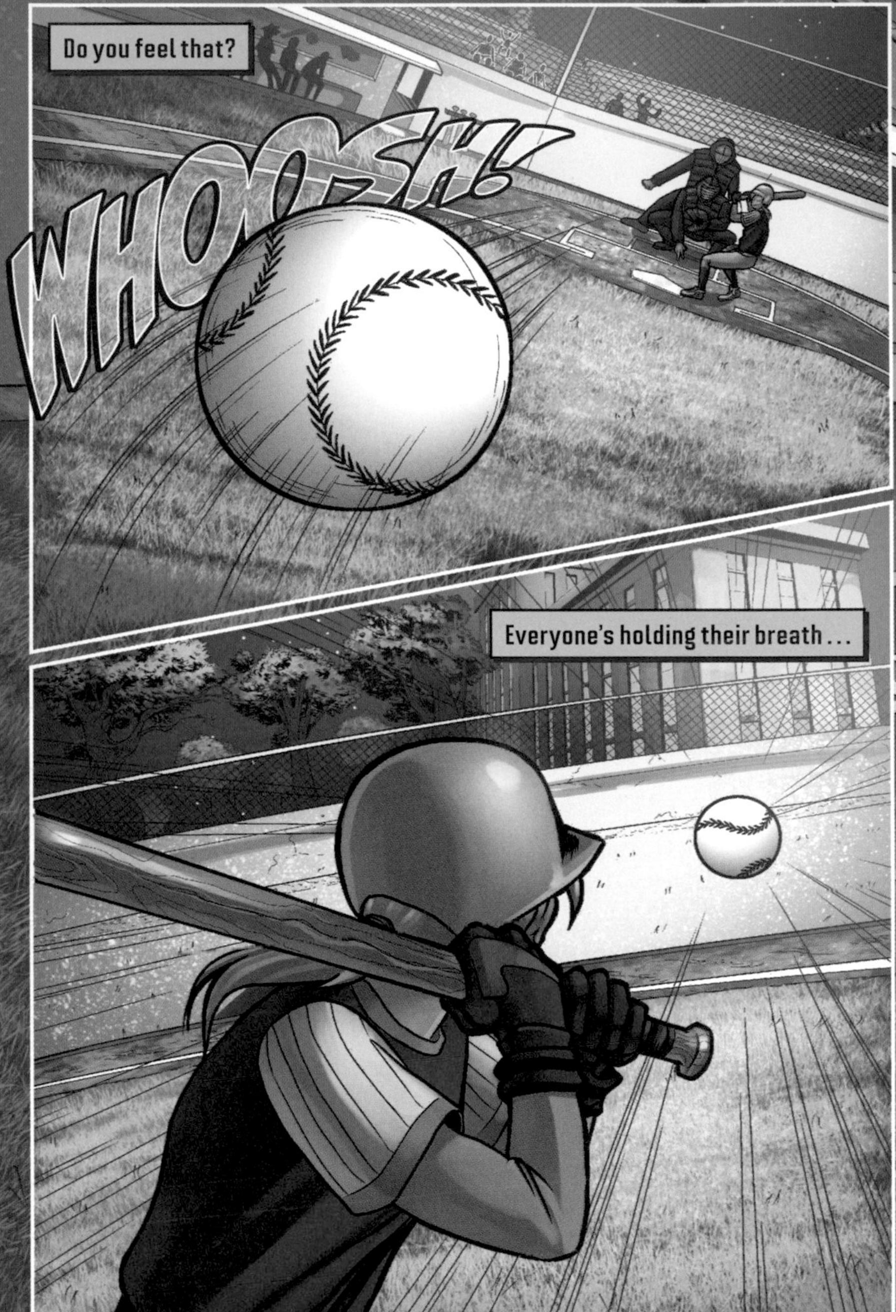
Do you feel that?
WHOOSH!
Everyone's holding their breath . . .

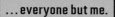
...everyone but me.

CRRACK!!

I'm Jake Thorson — the team captain of the Vikings and the best power hitter in the league.

That's Stormbreaker, my dad's old bat.

I'd be nothing without it.

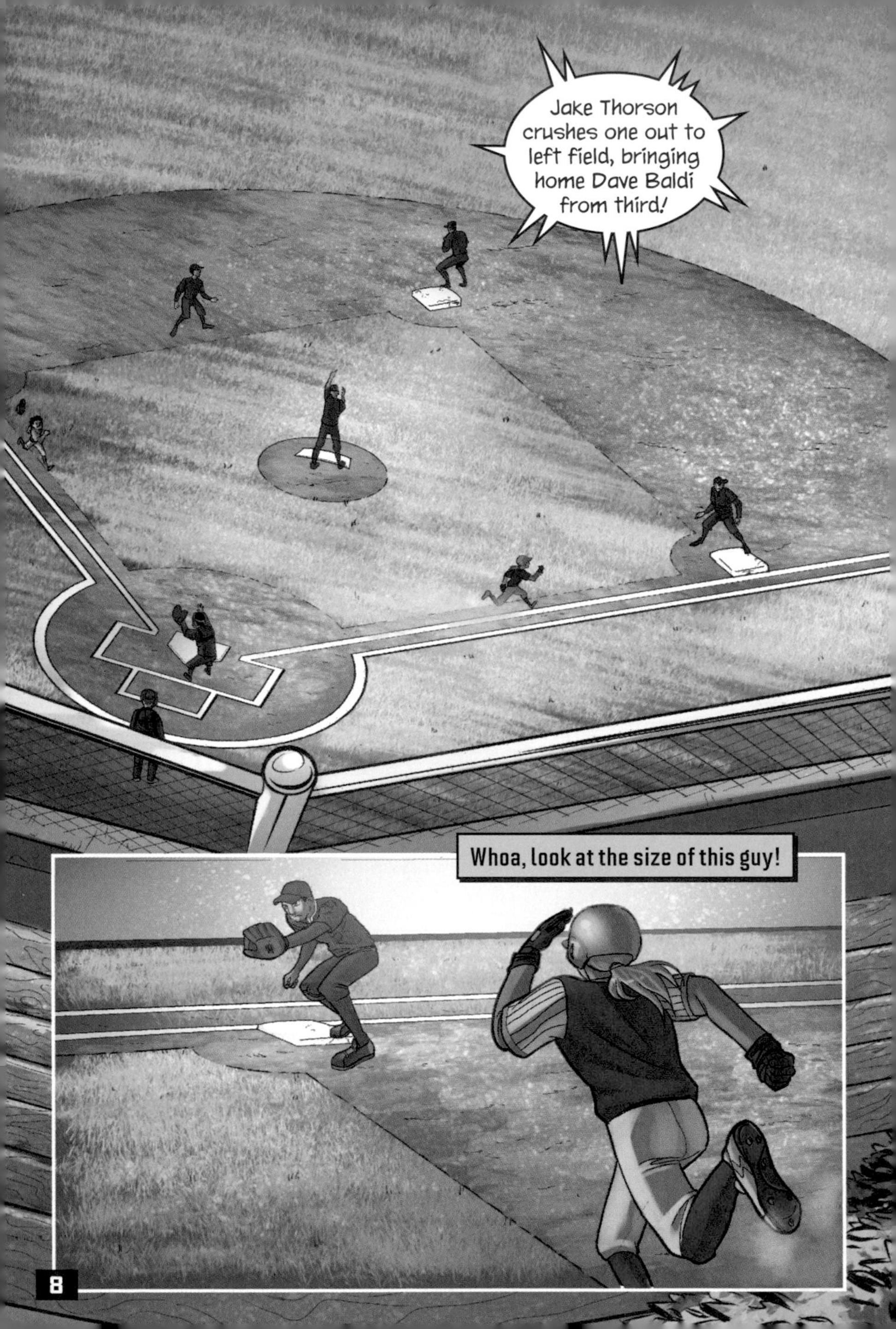
Jake Thorson crushes one out to left field, bringing home Dave Baldi from third!
Whoa, look at the size of this guy!

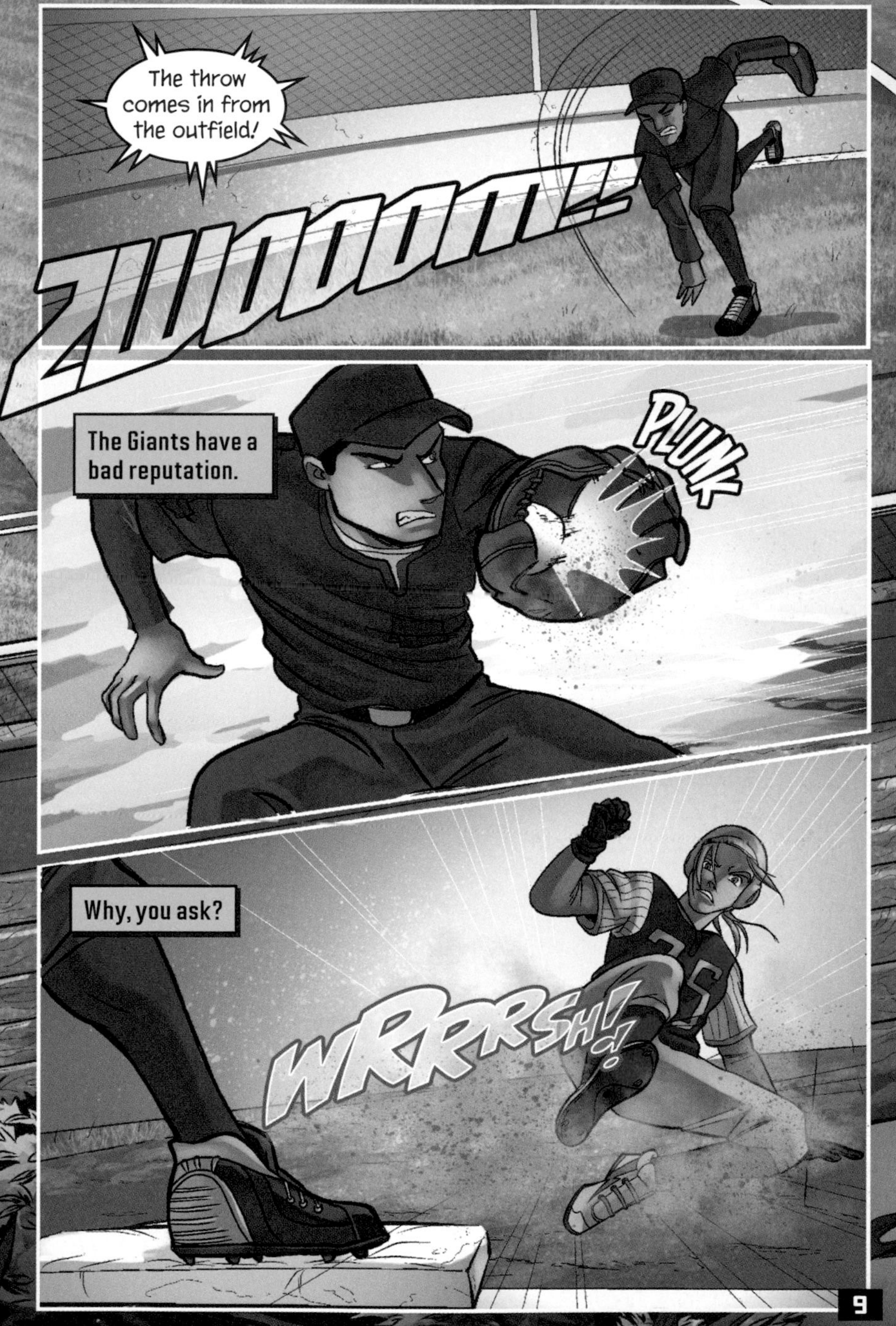
The throw comes in from the outfield!
ZWOOOM!!
The Giants have a bad reputation.
PLUNK
Why, you ask?
WRRRSH!

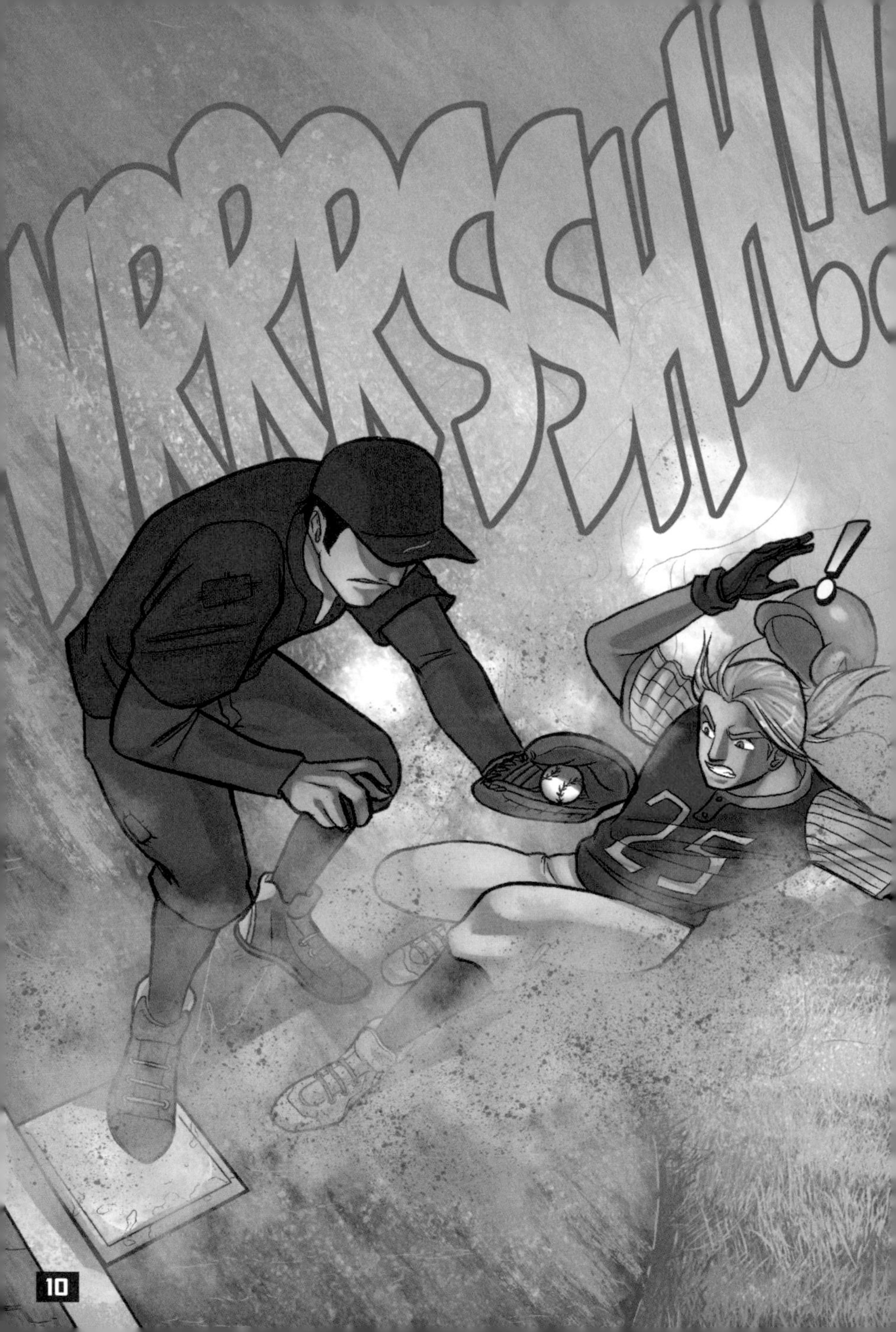

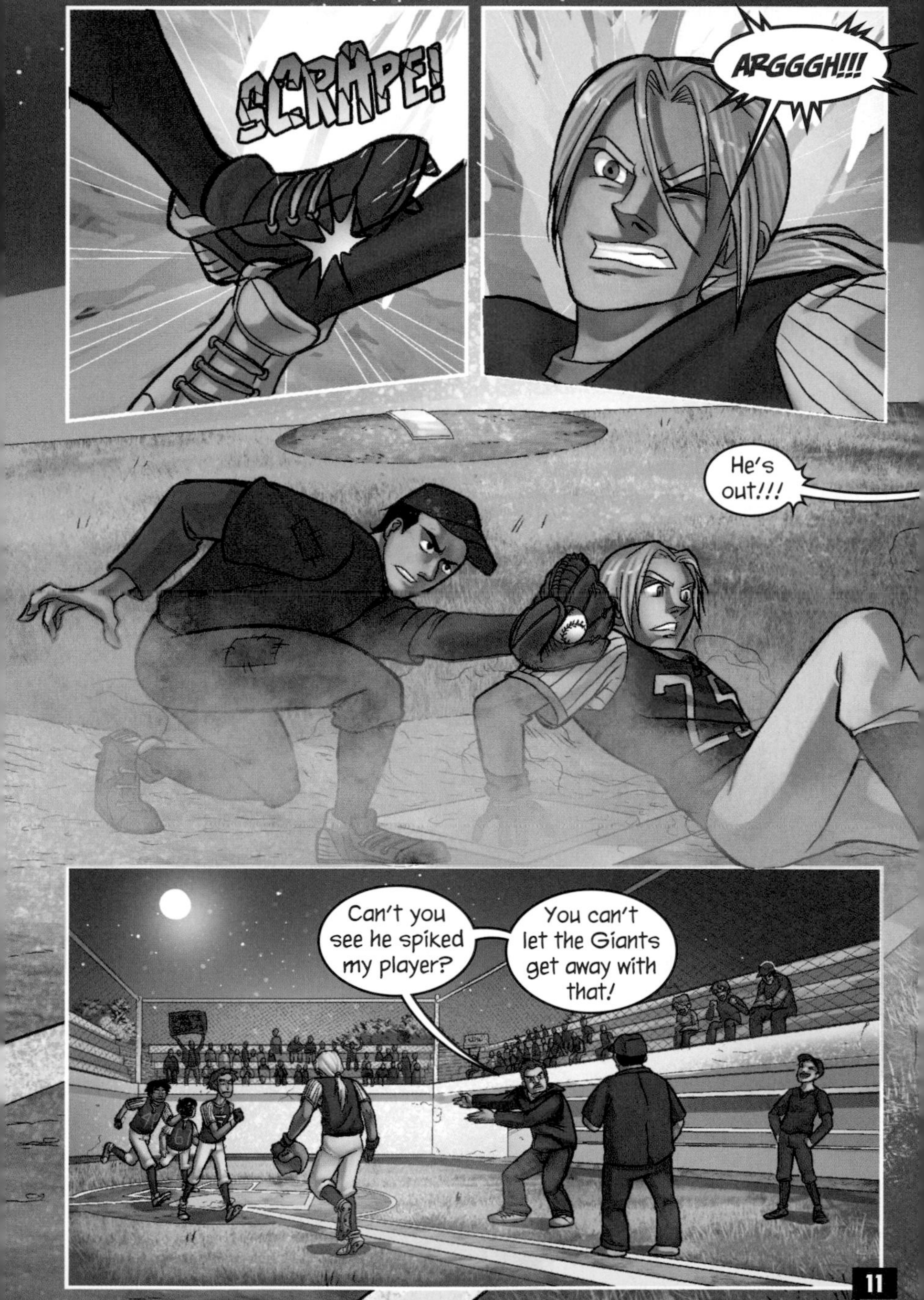
SCRAPE!
ARGGGH!!!
He's out!!!
Can't you see he spiked my player?
You can't let the Giants get away with that!

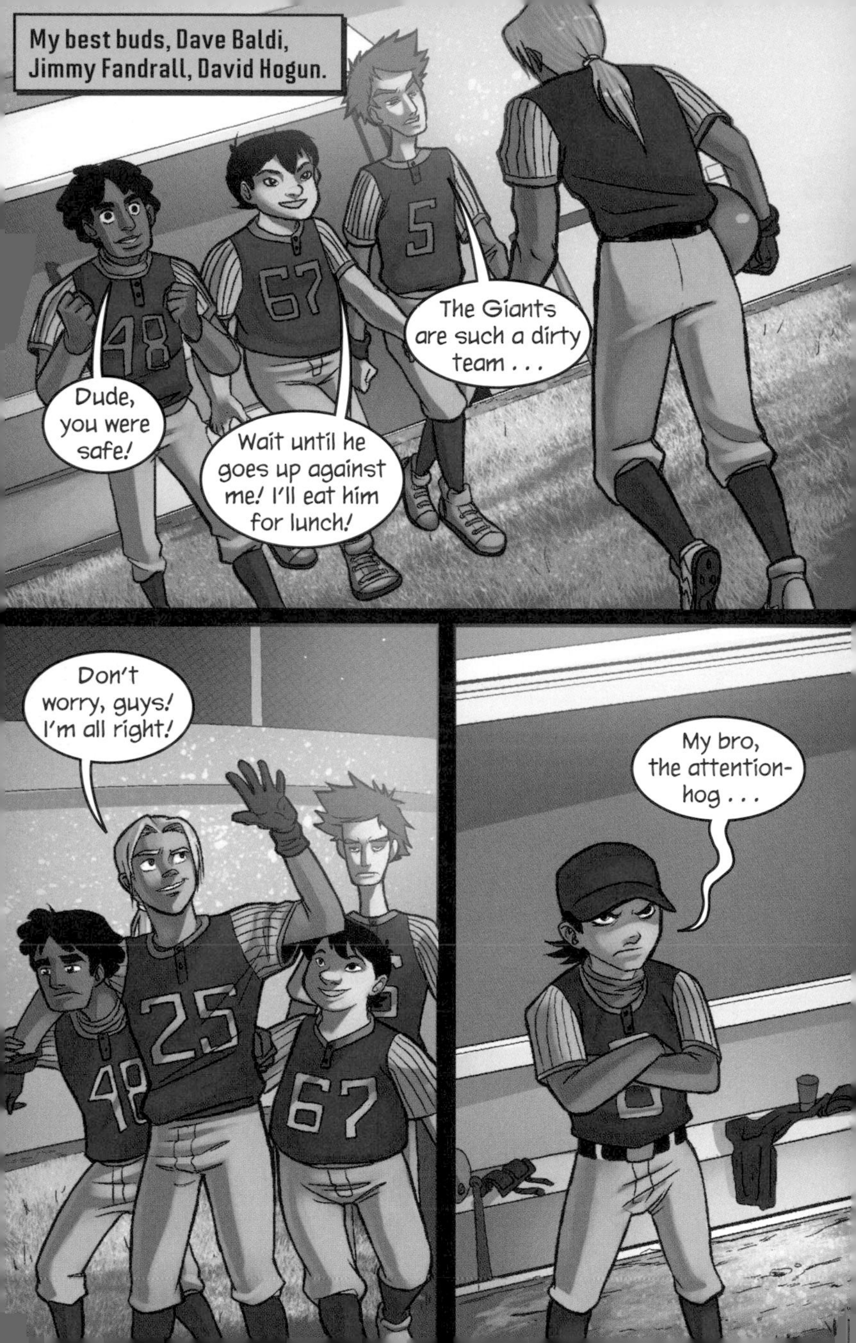

My best buds, Dave Baldi, Jimmy Fandrall, David Hogun.
Dude, you were safe!
Wait until he goes up against me! I'll eat him for lunch!
The Giants are such a dirty team . . .
Don't worry, guys! I'm all right!
My bro, the attention-hog . . .

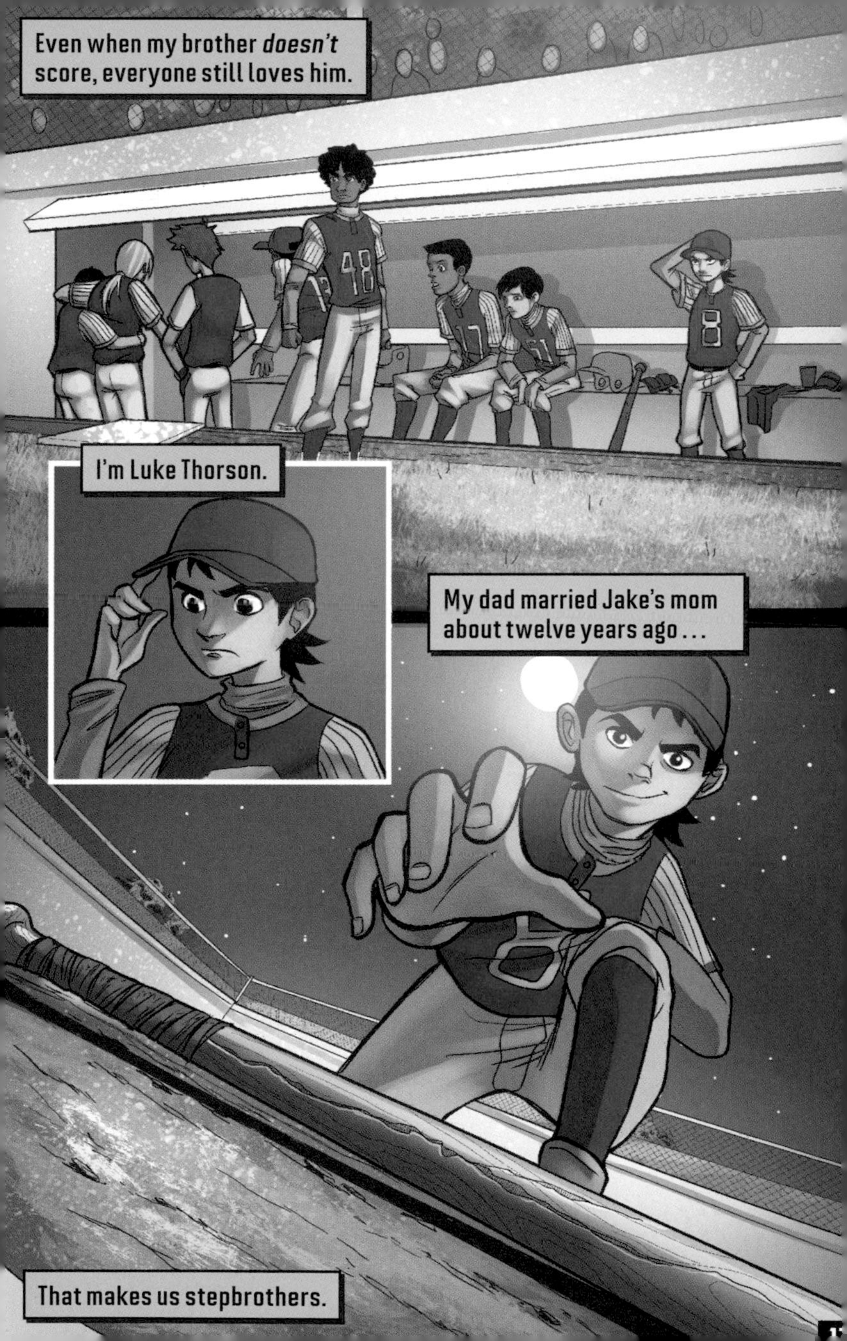
Even when my brother *doesn't* score, everyone still loves him.
I'm Luke Thorson.
My dad married Jake's mom about twelve years ago . . .
That makes us stepbrothers.

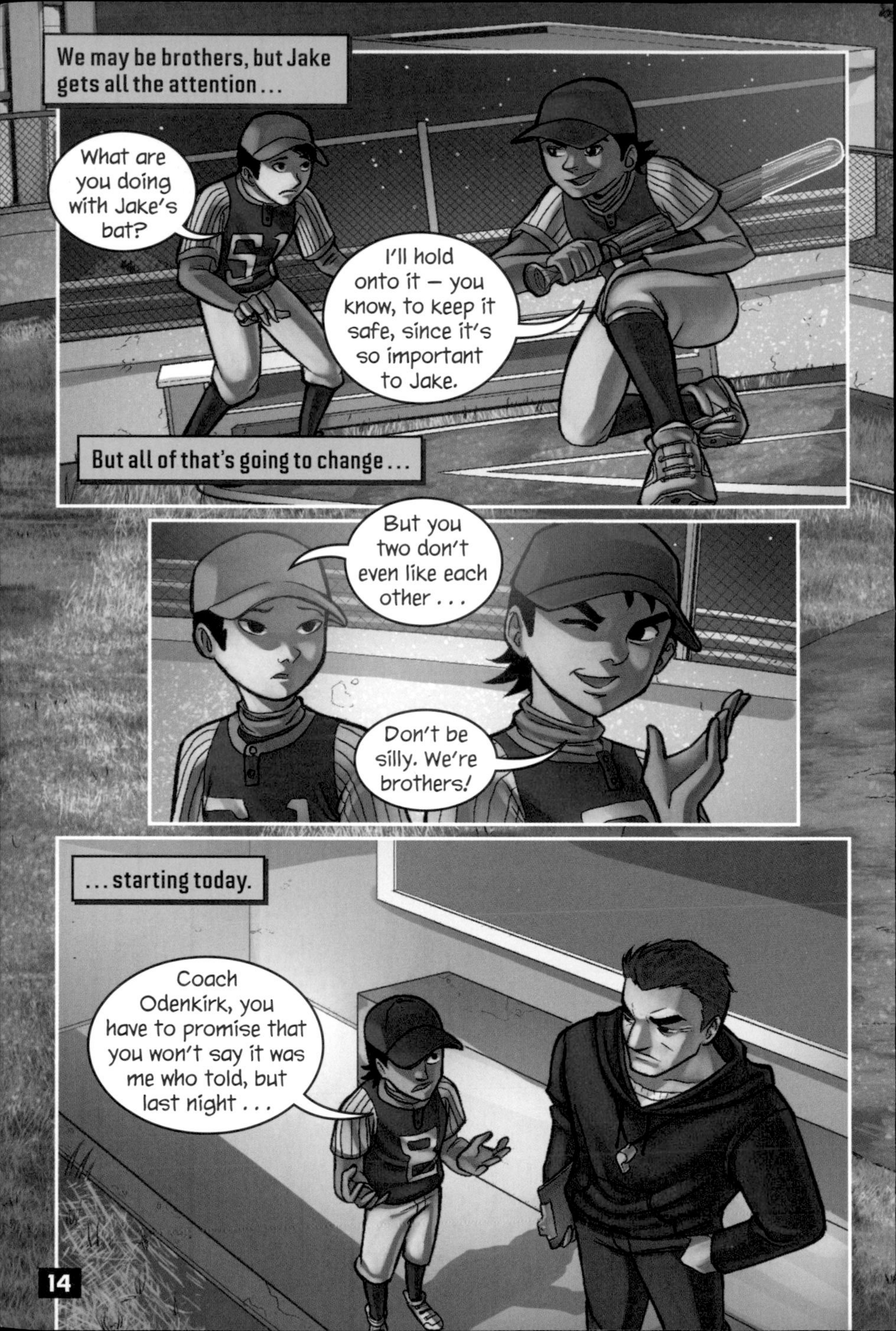

We may be brothers, but Jake gets all the attention . . .
What are you doing with Jake's bat?
I'll hold onto it — you know, to keep it safe, since it's so important to Jake.
But all of that's going to change . . .
But you two don't even like each other . . .
Don't be silly. We're brothers!
. . . starting today.
Coach Odenkirk, you have to promise that you won't say it was me who told, but last night . . .

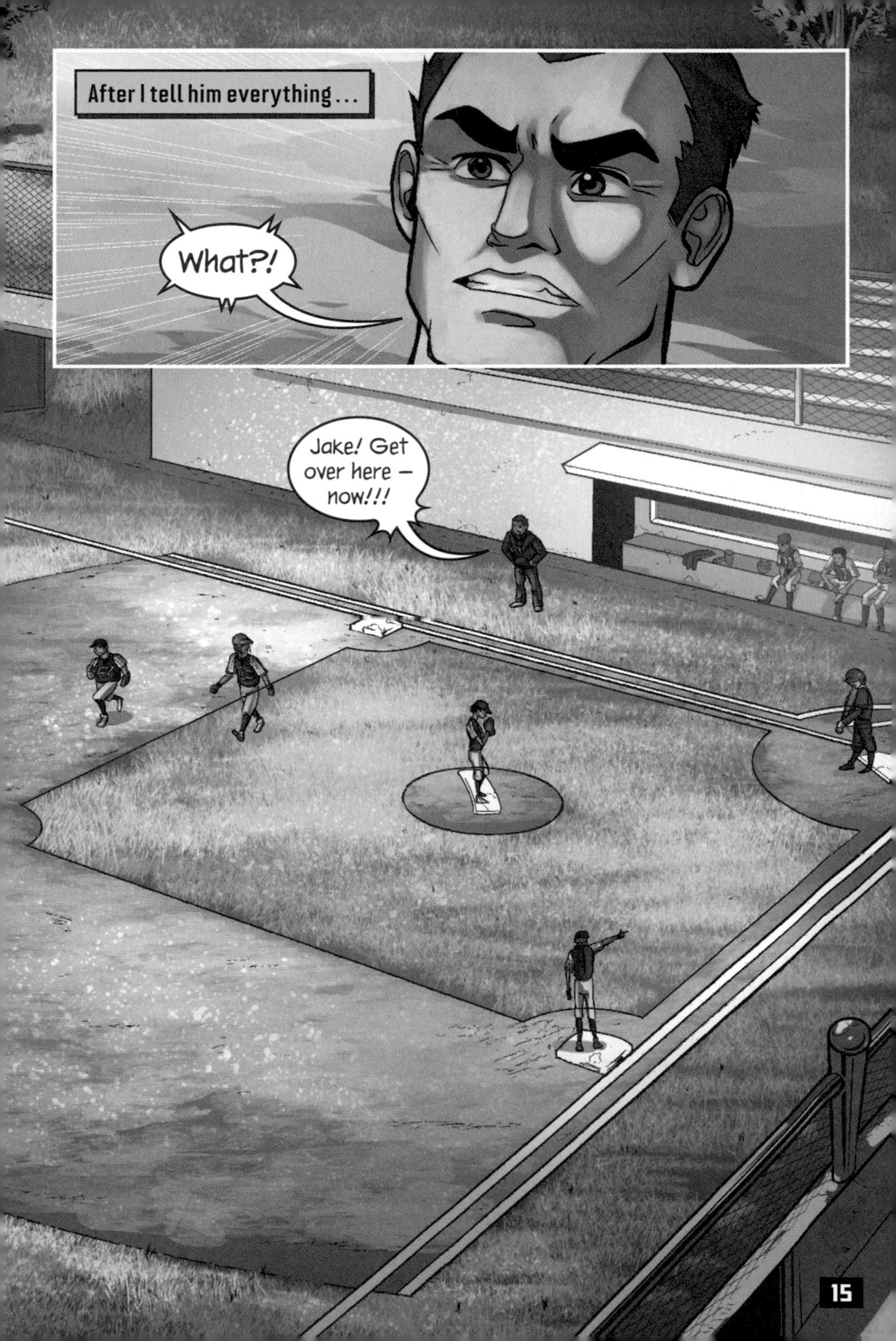
After I tell him everything . . .
What?!
Jake! Get over here — now!!!

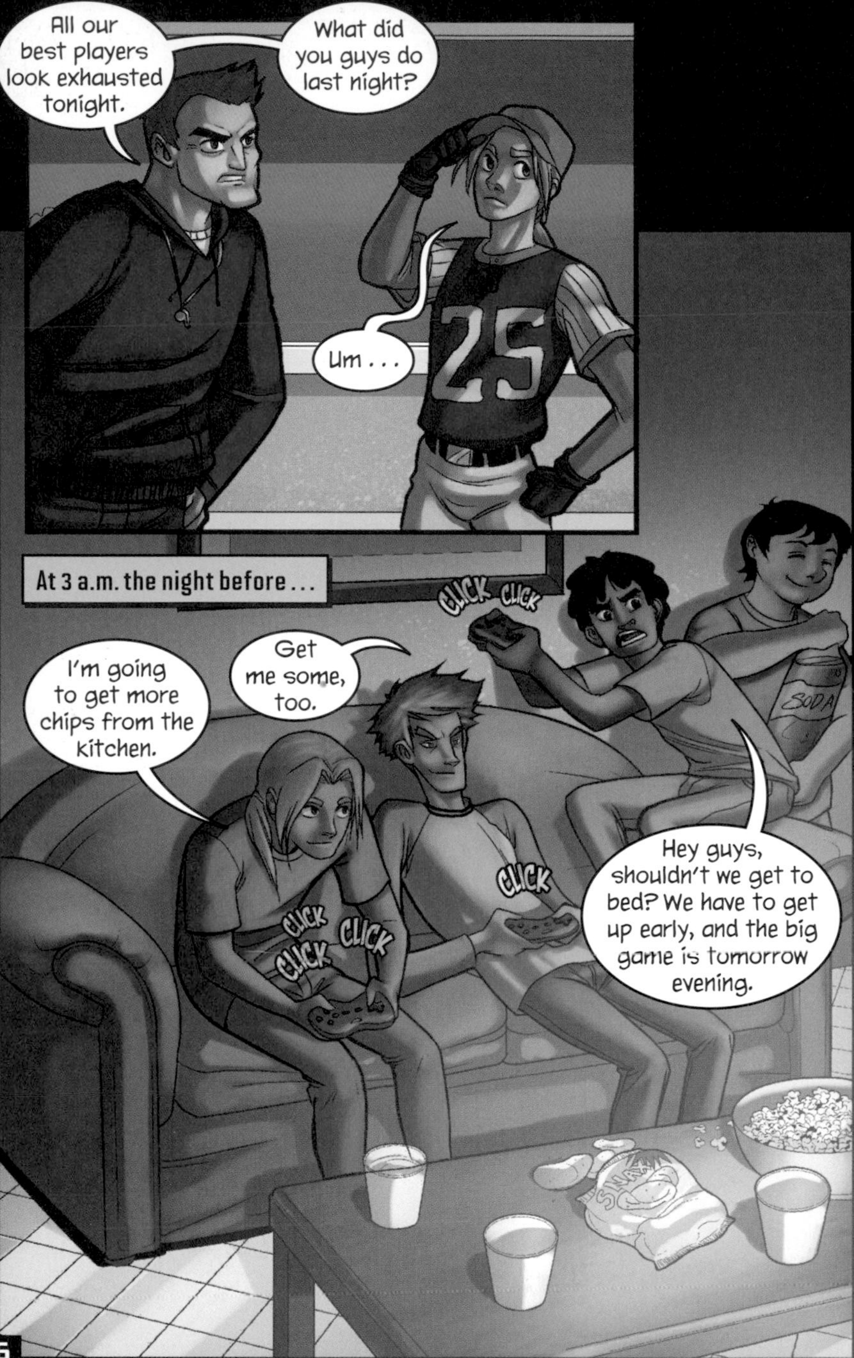
All our best players look exhausted tonight.
What did you guys do last night?
Um . . .
At 3 a.m. the night before . . .
CLICK CLICK
I'm going to get more chips from the kitchen.
Get me some, too.
CLICK
CLICK CLICK CLICK
Hey guys, shouldn't we get to bed? We have to get up early, and the big game is tomorrow evening.
SODA

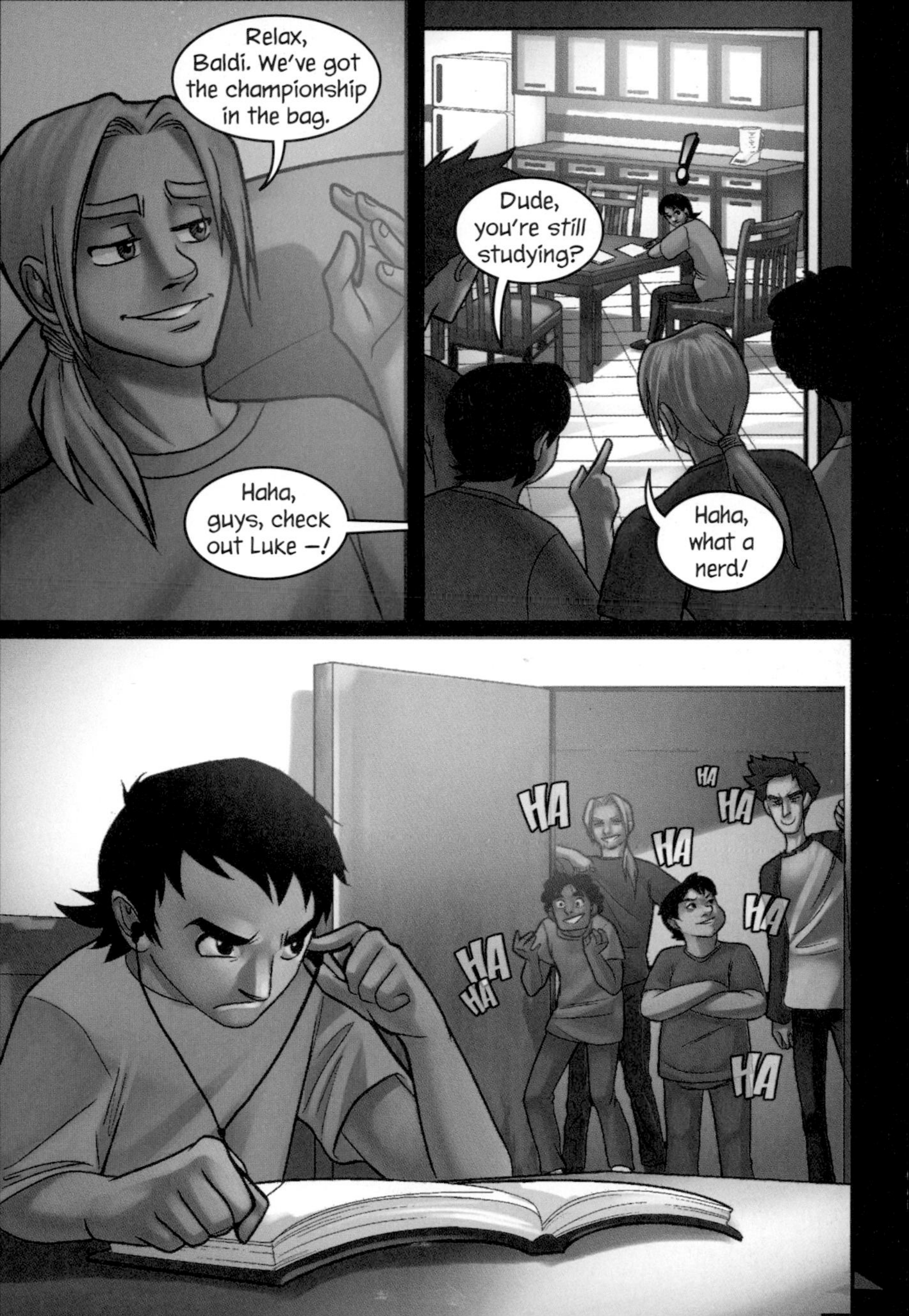
Relax, Baldi. We've got the championship in the bag.
Haha, guys, check out Luke –!
!
Dude, you're still studying?
Haha, what a nerd!
HA
HA
HA
HA
HA
HA
HA
HA

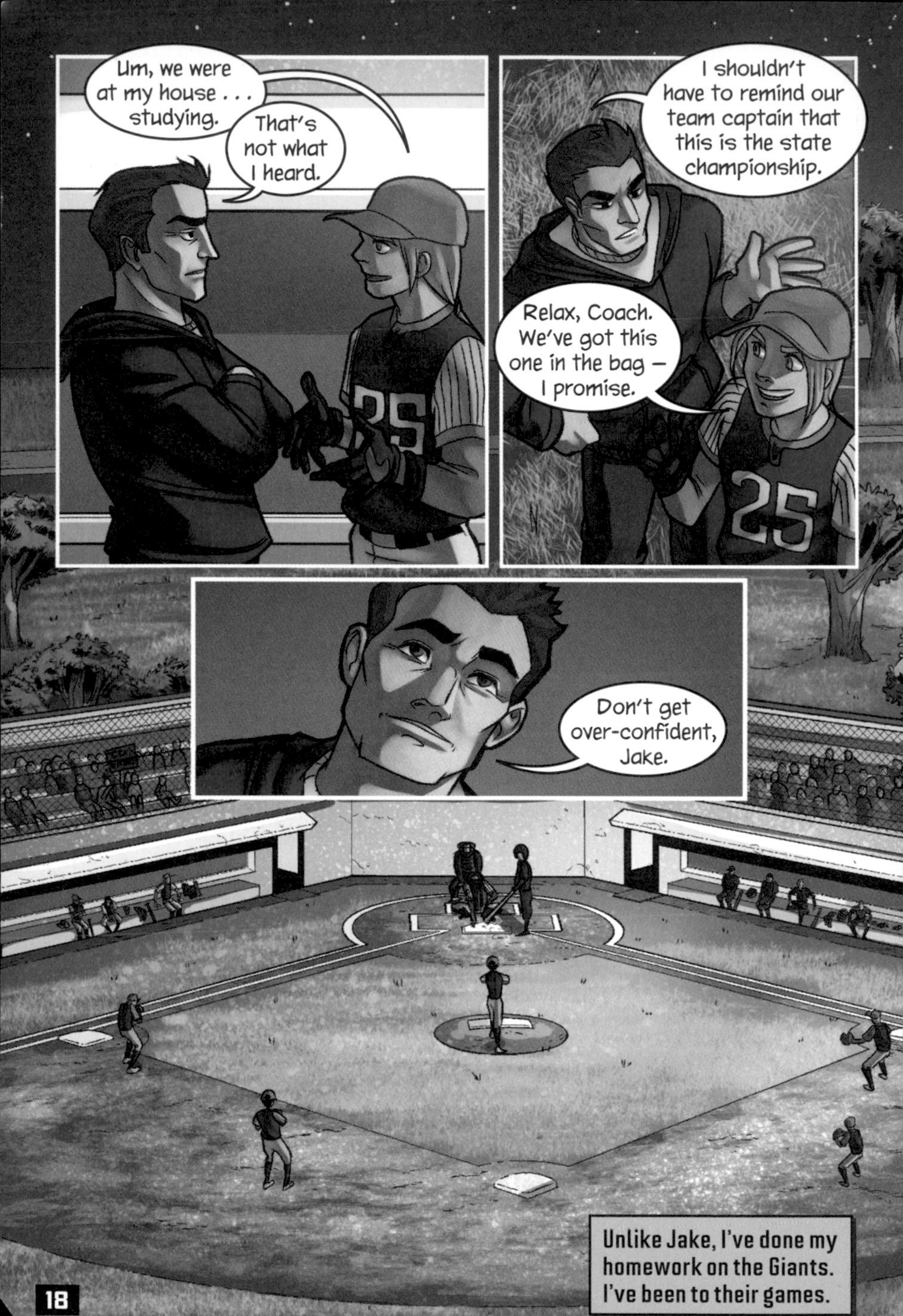
Um, we were at my house . . . studying.
That's not what I heard.
I shouldn't have to remind our team captain that this is the state championship.
Relax, Coach. We've got this one in the bag — I promise.
Don't get over-confident, Jake.
Unlike Jake, I've done my homework on the Giants. I've been to their games.

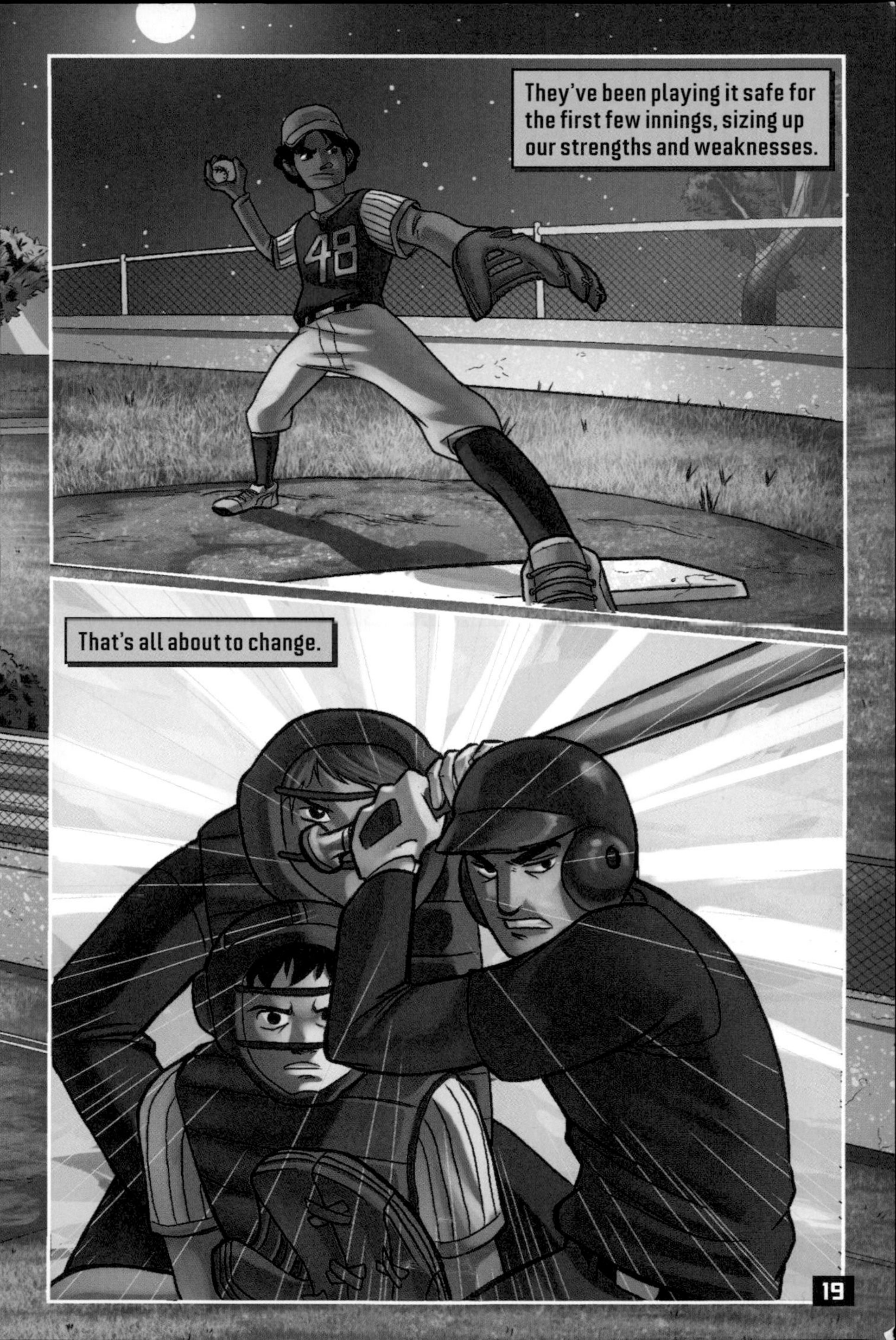
They've been playing it safe for the first few innings, sizing up our strengths and weaknesses.
48
That's all about to change.

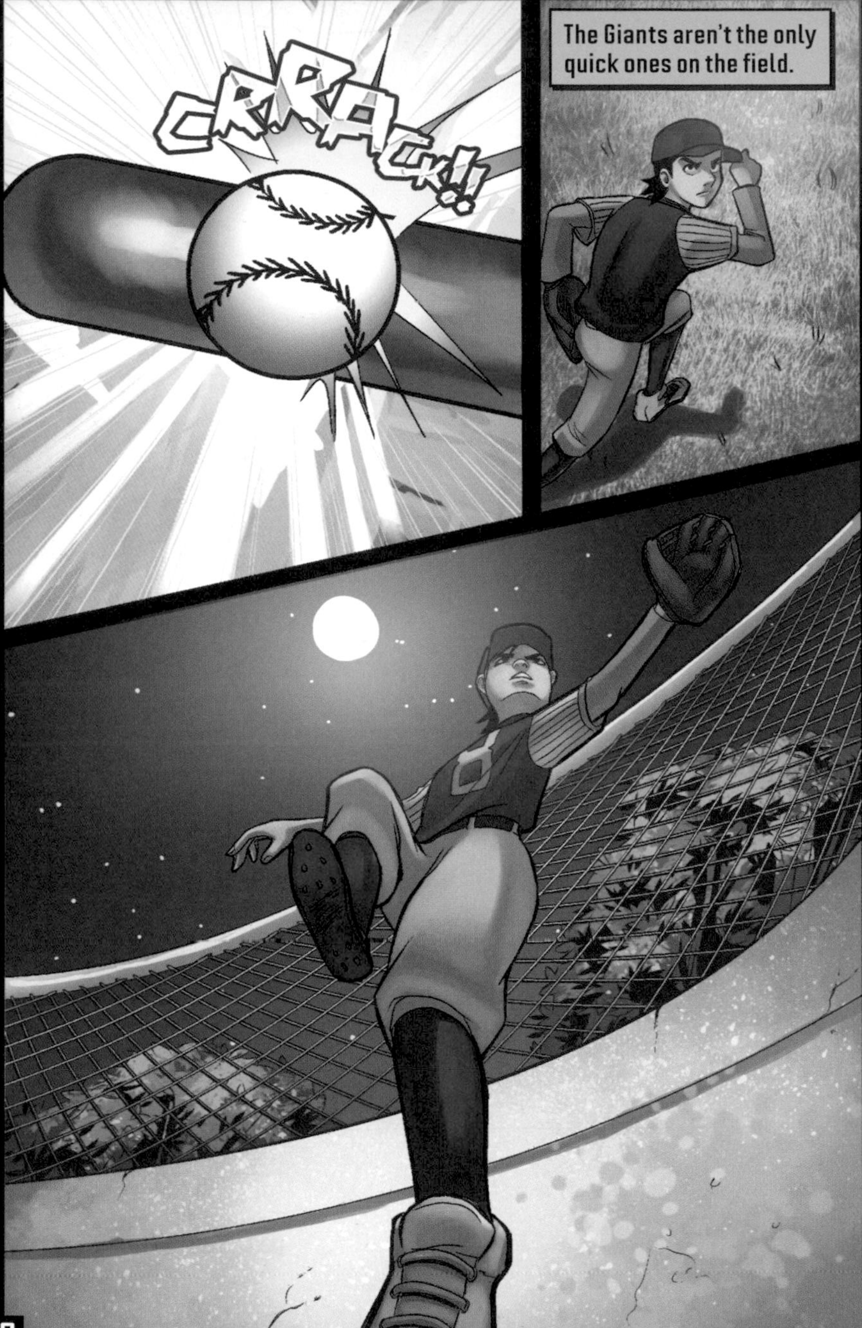
CRRACK!!
The Giants aren't the only quick ones on the field.

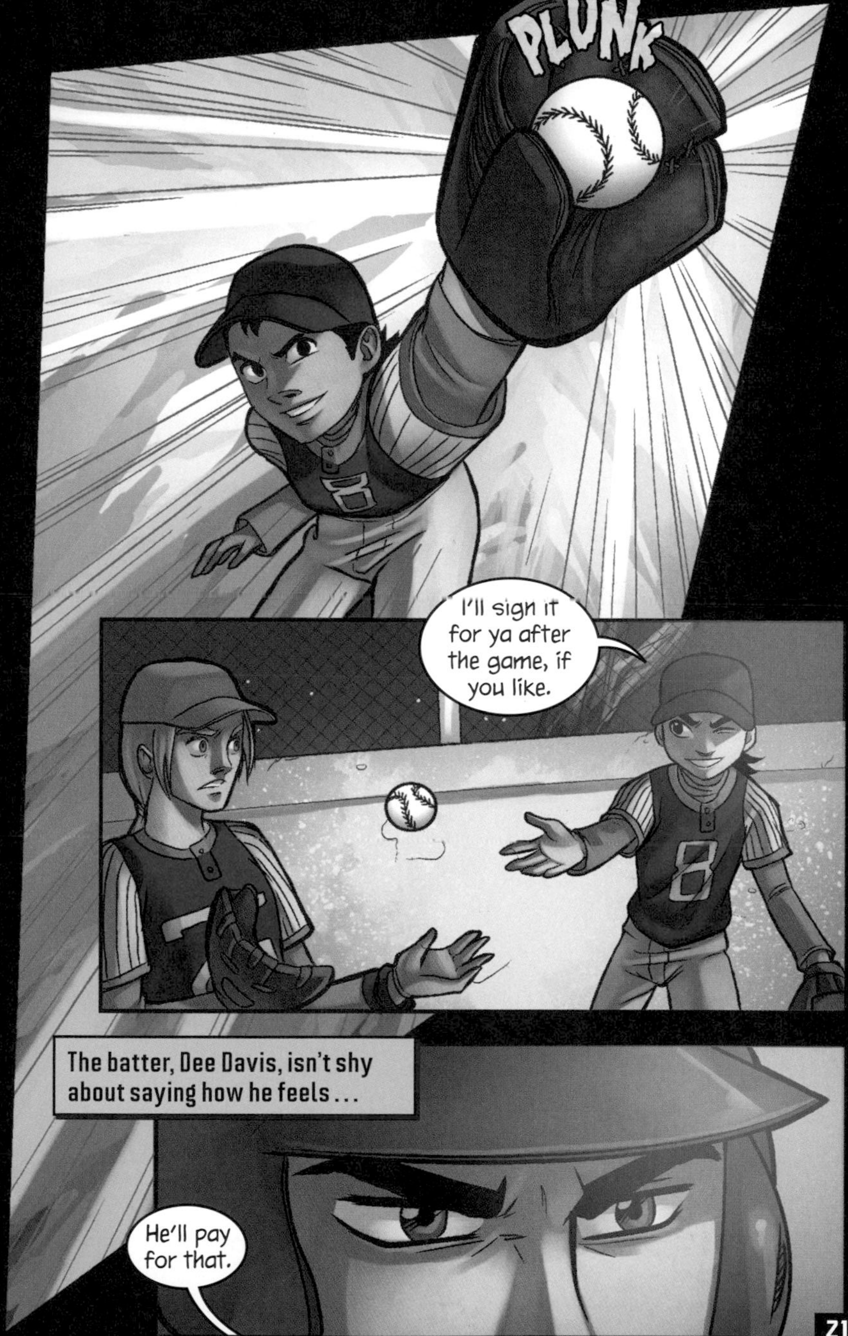
PLUNK
I'll sign it for ya after the game, if you like.
The batter, Dee Davis, isn't shy about saying how he feels . . .
He'll pay for that.

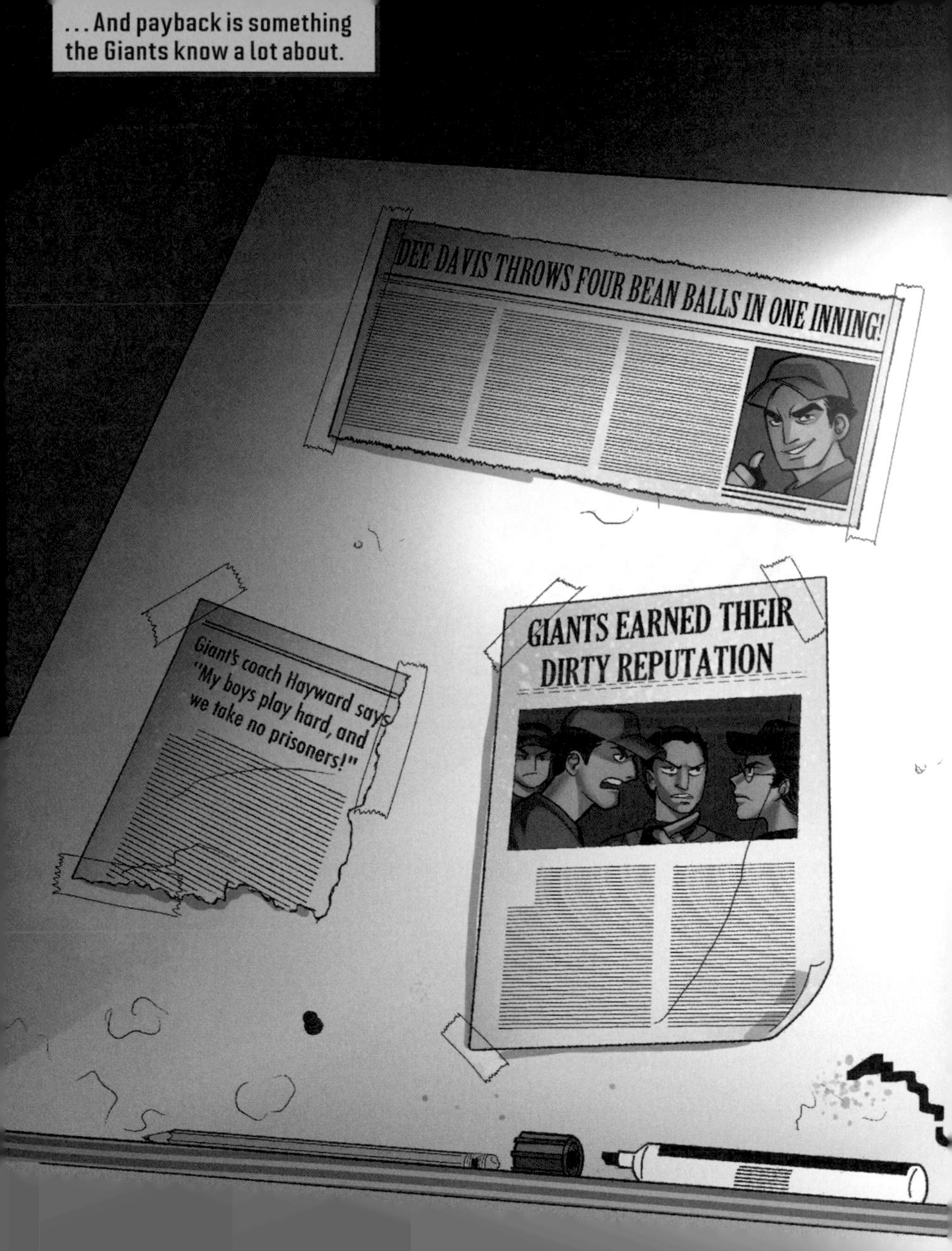

. . . And payback is something the Giants know a lot about.
DEE DAVIS THROWS FOUR BEAN BALLS IN ONE INNING!
Giant's coach Hayward says "My boys play hard, and we take no prisoners!"
GIANTS EARNED THEIR DIRTY REPUTATION

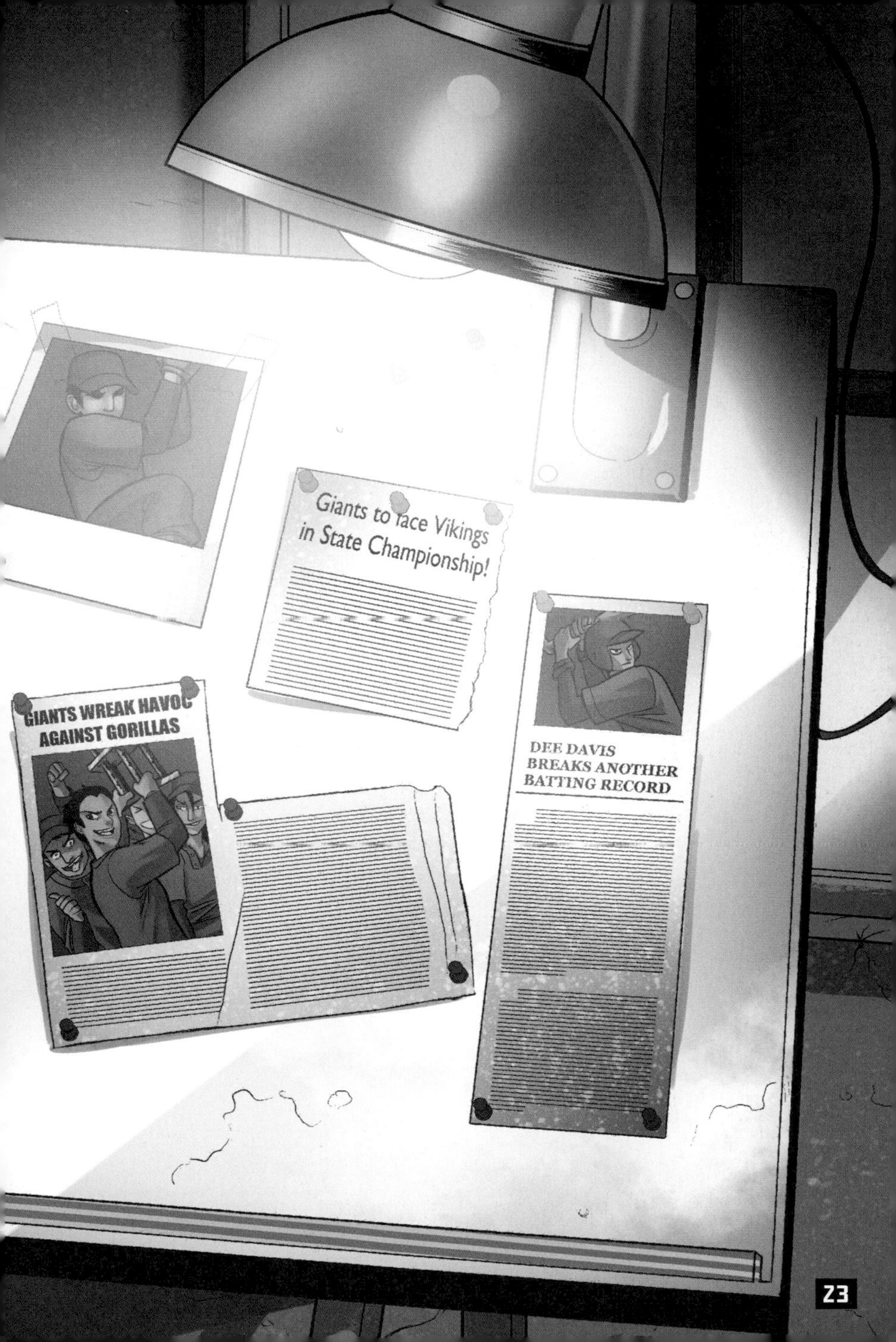
Giants to face Vikings in State Championship!
GIANTS WREAK HAVOC AGAINST GORILLAS
DEE DAVIS BREAKS ANOTHER BATTING RECORD

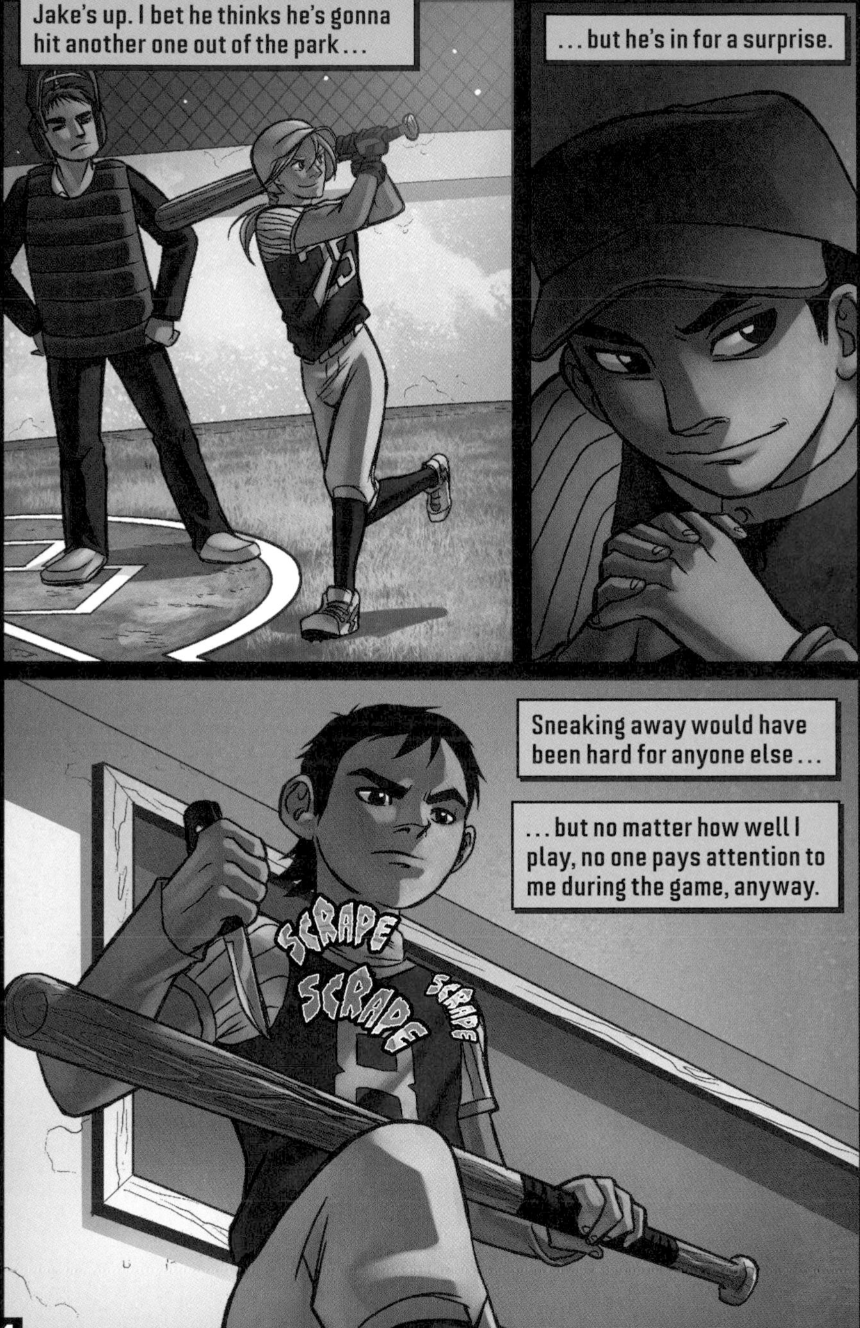
Jake's up. I bet he thinks he's gonna hit another one out of the park . . .
. . . but he's in for a surprise.
Sneaking away would have been hard for anyone else . . .
. . . but no matter how well I play, no one pays attention to me during the game, anyway.
SCRAPE
SCRAPE
SCRAPE

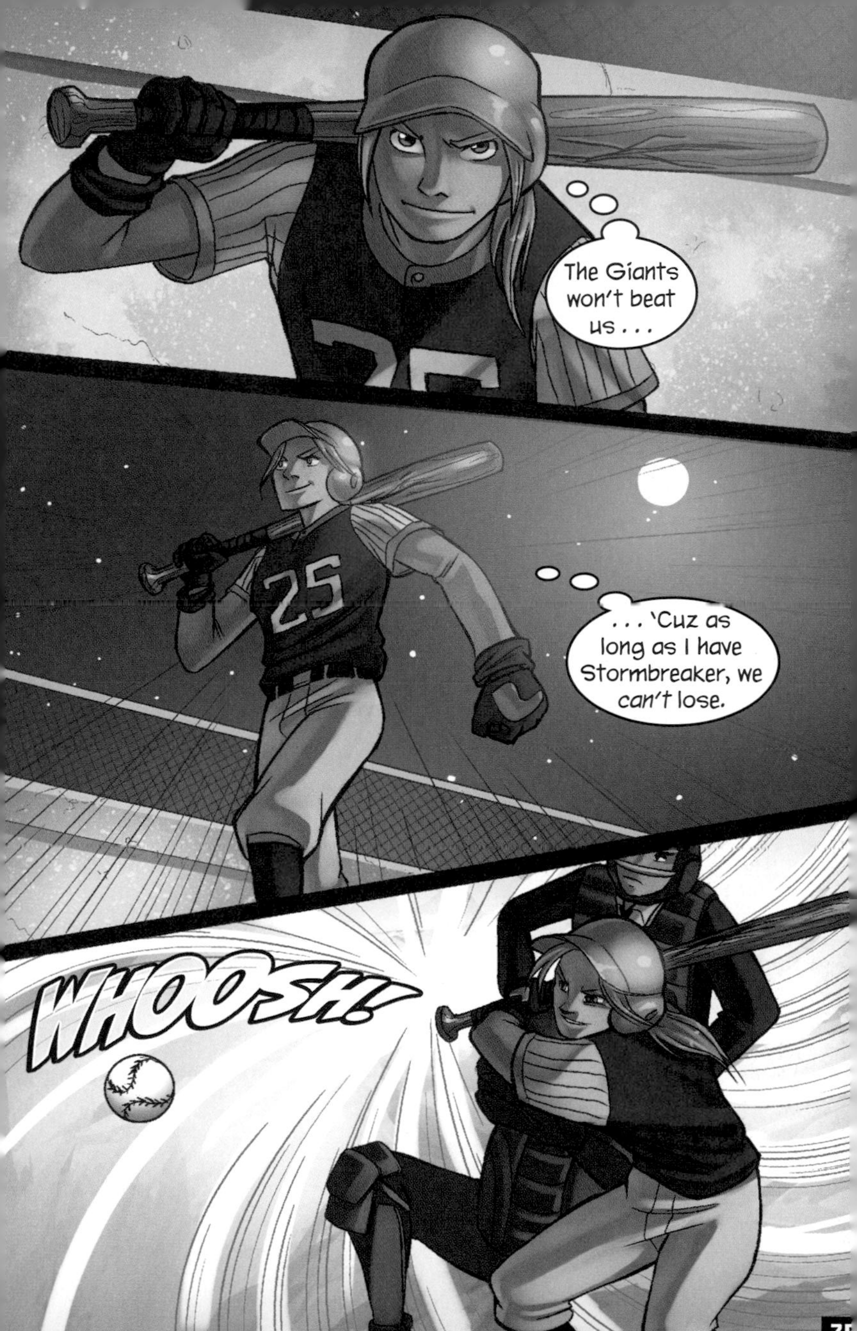
The Giants won't beat us . . .
. . . 'Cuz as long as I have Stormbreaker, we can't lose.
WHOOSH!

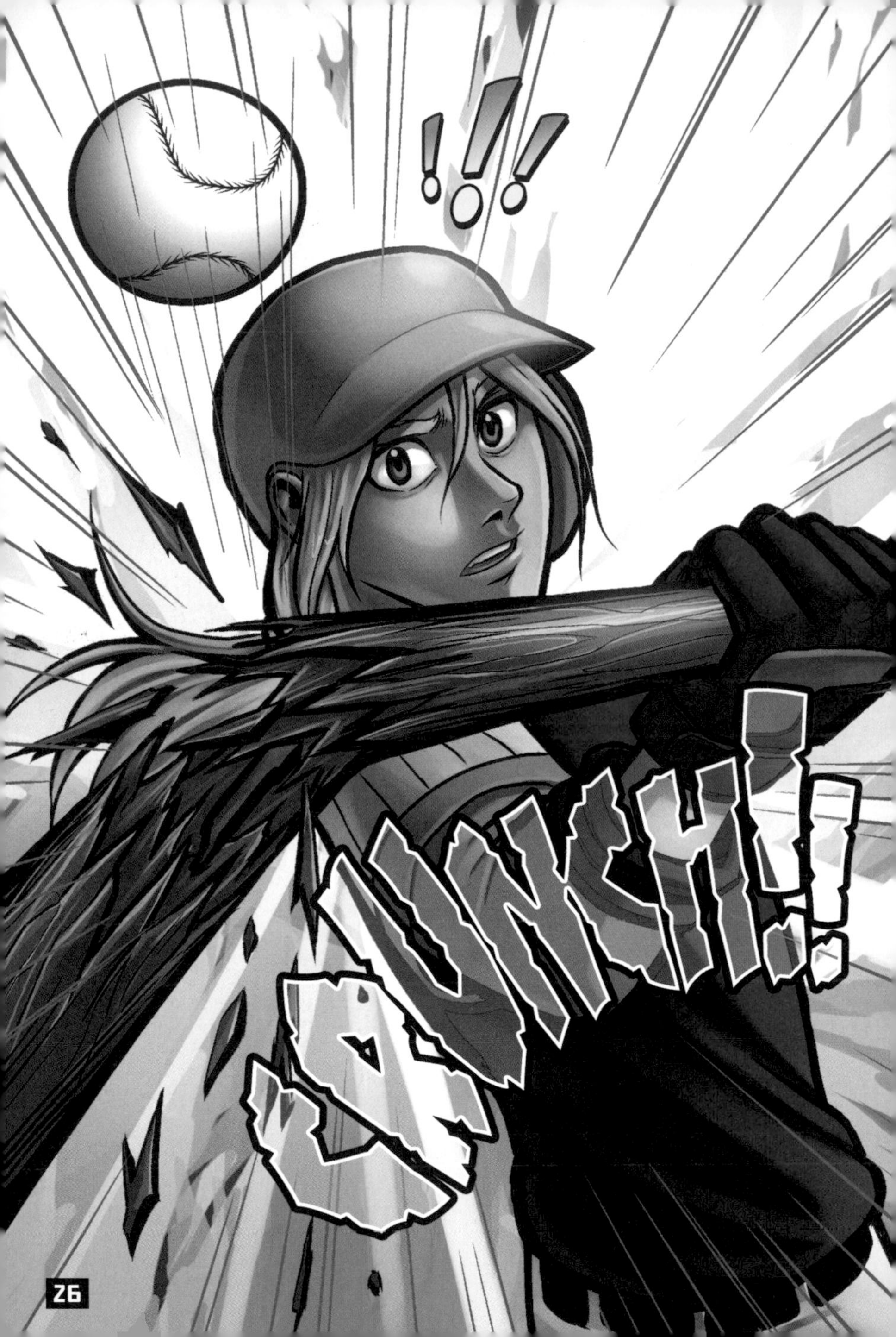
!!!
CRUNCH!!

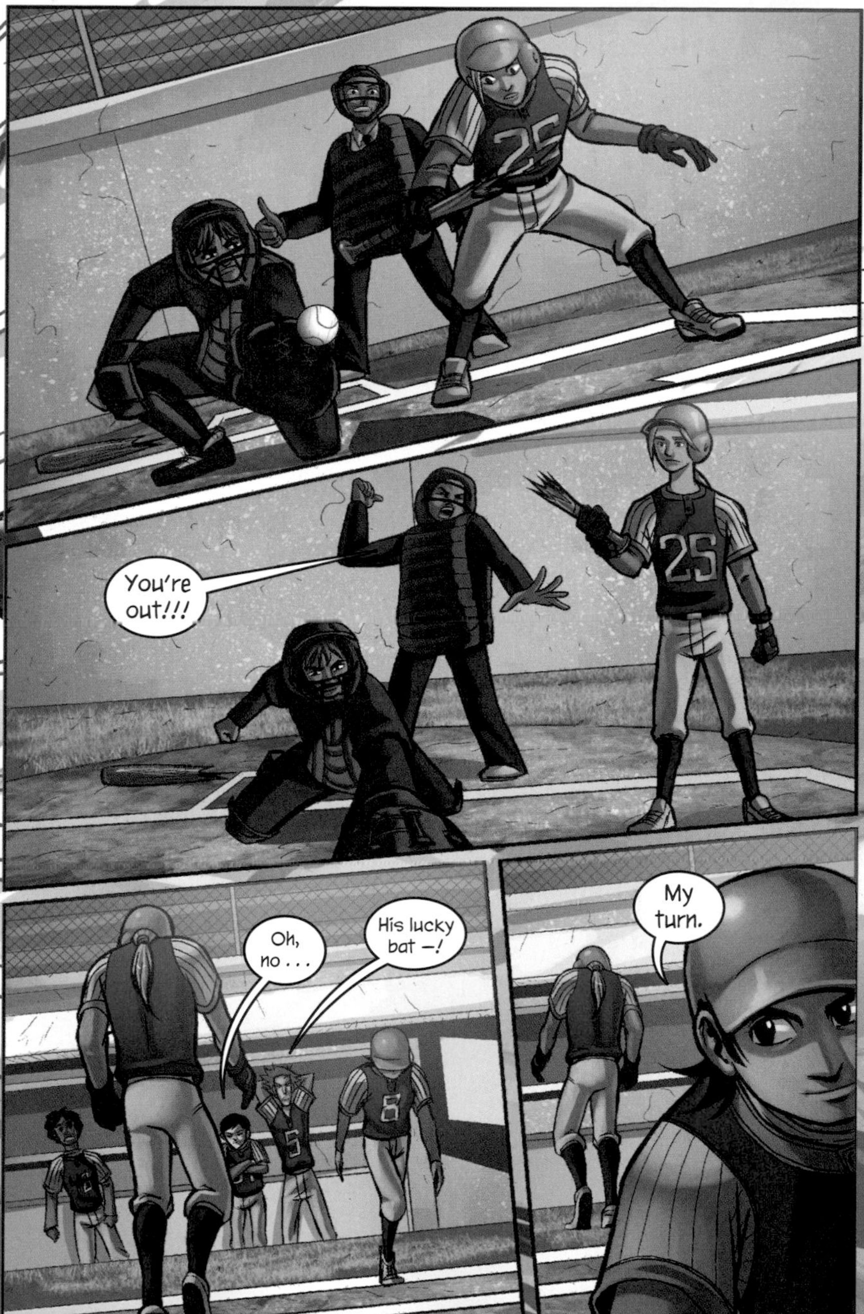
You're out!!!
Oh, no . . .
His lucky bat —!
My turn.

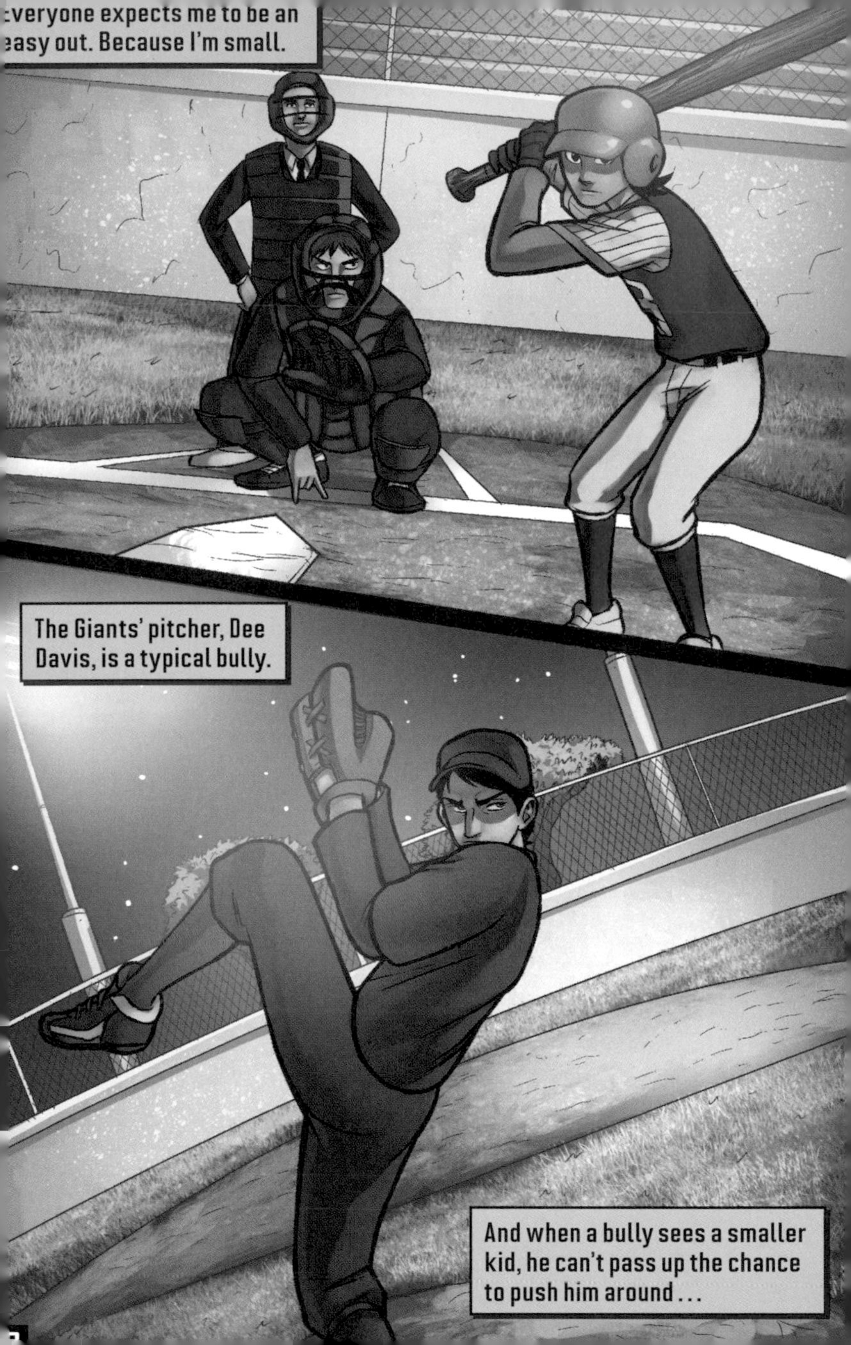

Everyone expects me to be an easy out. Because I'm small.
The Giants' pitcher, Dee Davis, is a typical bully.
And when a bully sees a smaller kid, he can't pass up the chance to push him around . . .

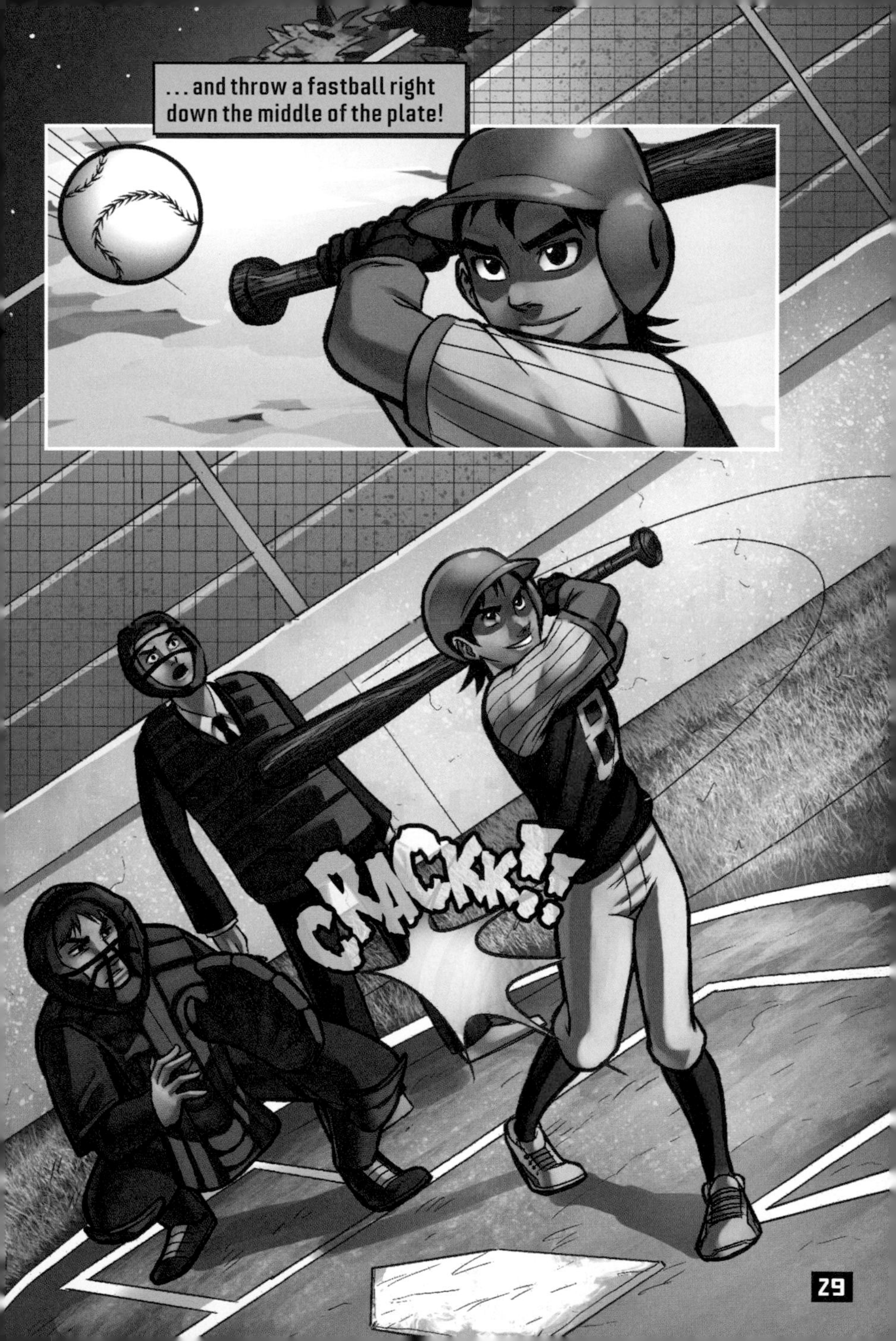
. . . and throw a fastball right down the middle of the plate!
CRACKK!!

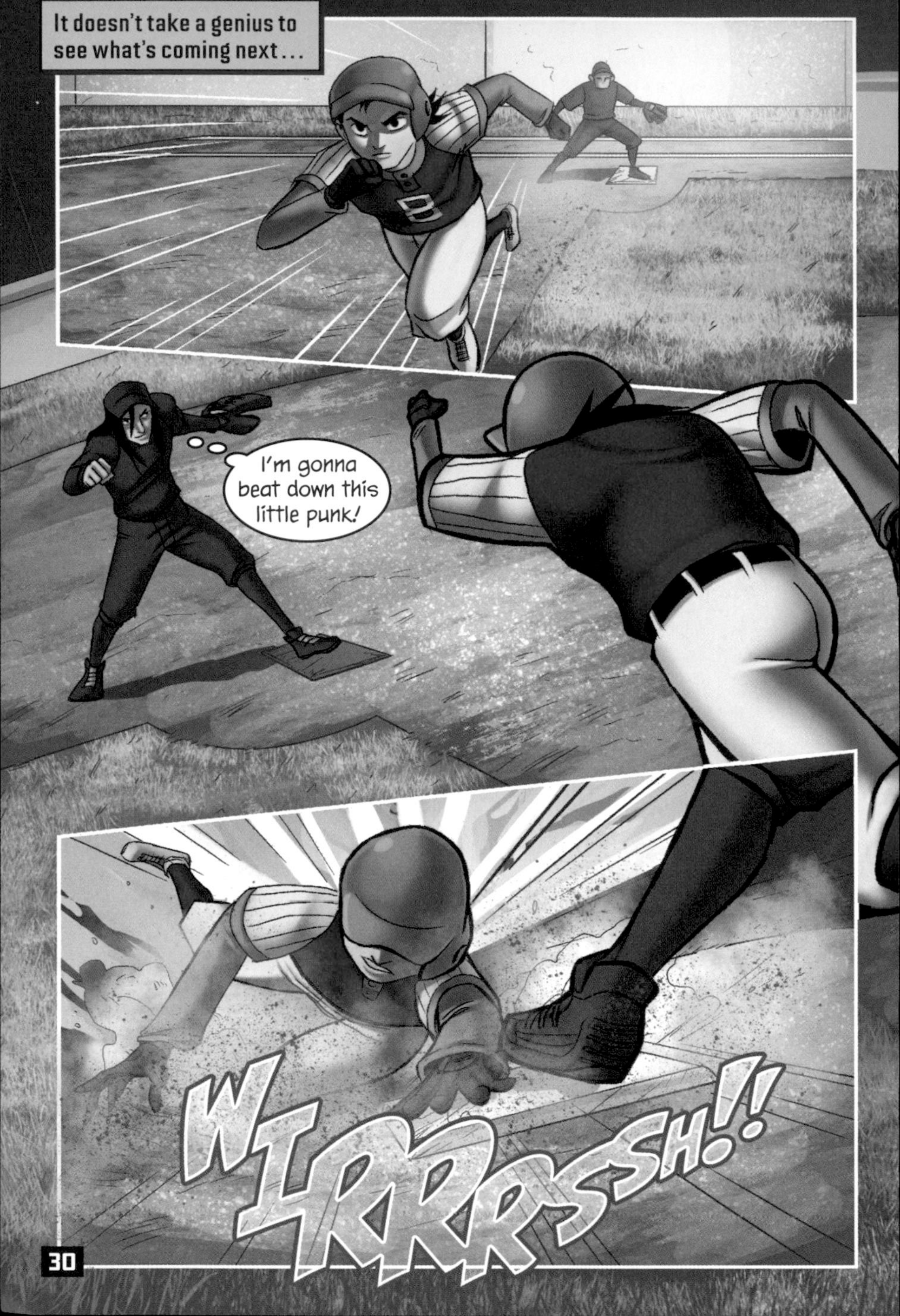
It doesn't take a genius to see what's coming next . . .
I'm gonna beat down this little punk!
WIRRRSSH!!

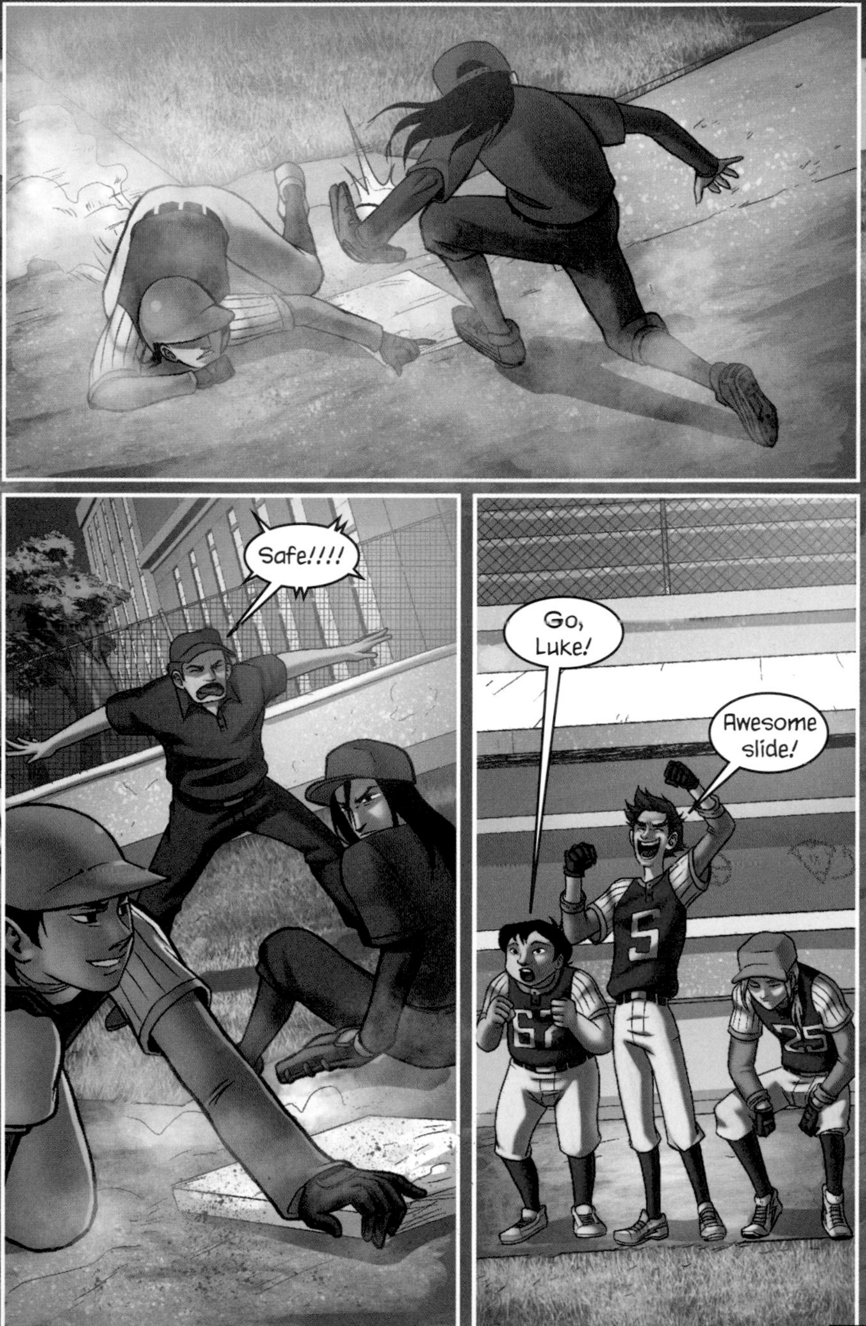
Safe!!!!
Go, Luke!
Awesome slide!

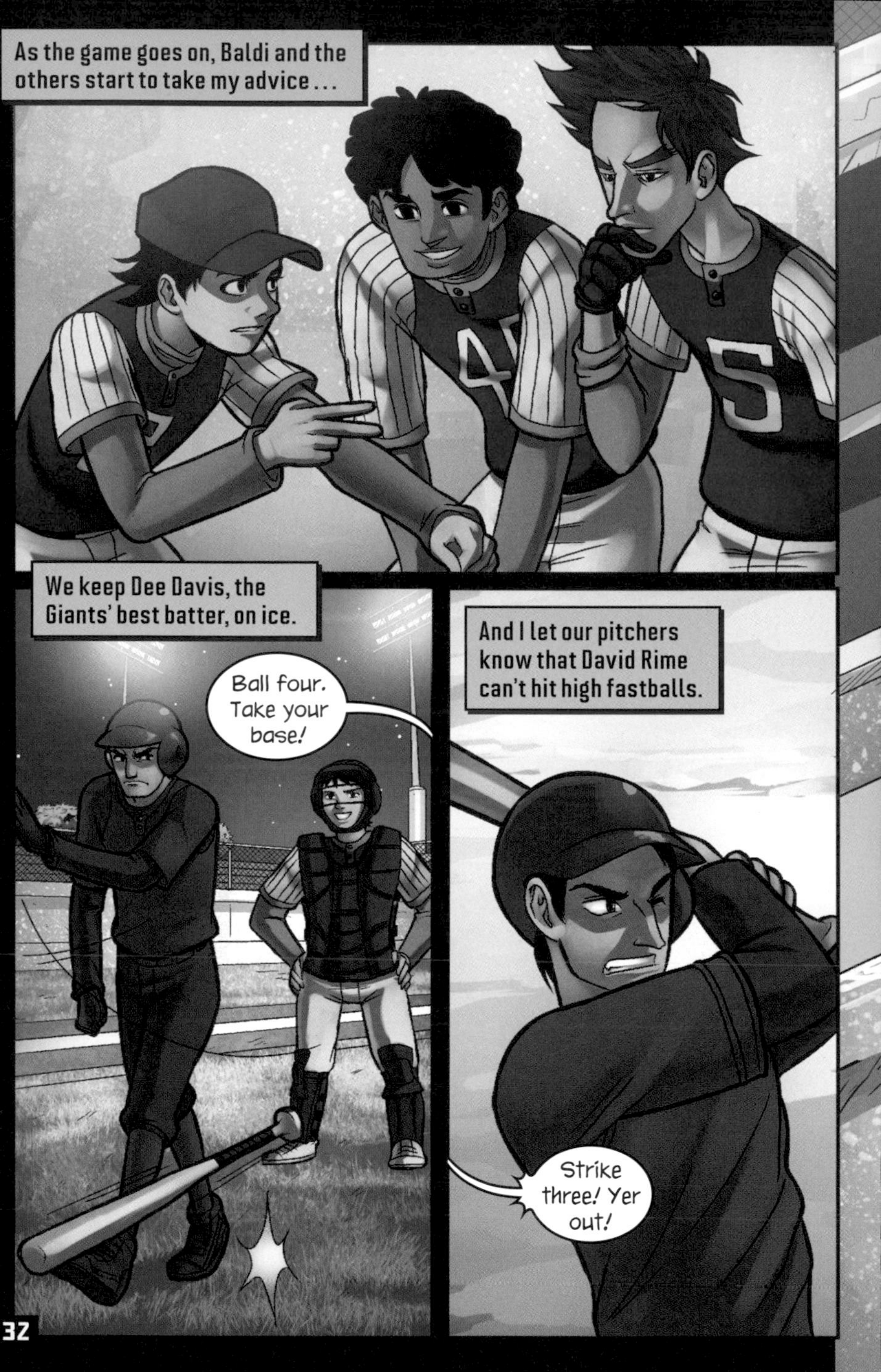
As the game goes on, Baldi and the others start to take my advice . . .
We keep Dee Davis, the Giants' best batter, on ice.
Ball four. Take your base!
And I let our pitchers know that David Rime can't hit high fastballs.
Strike three! Yer out!

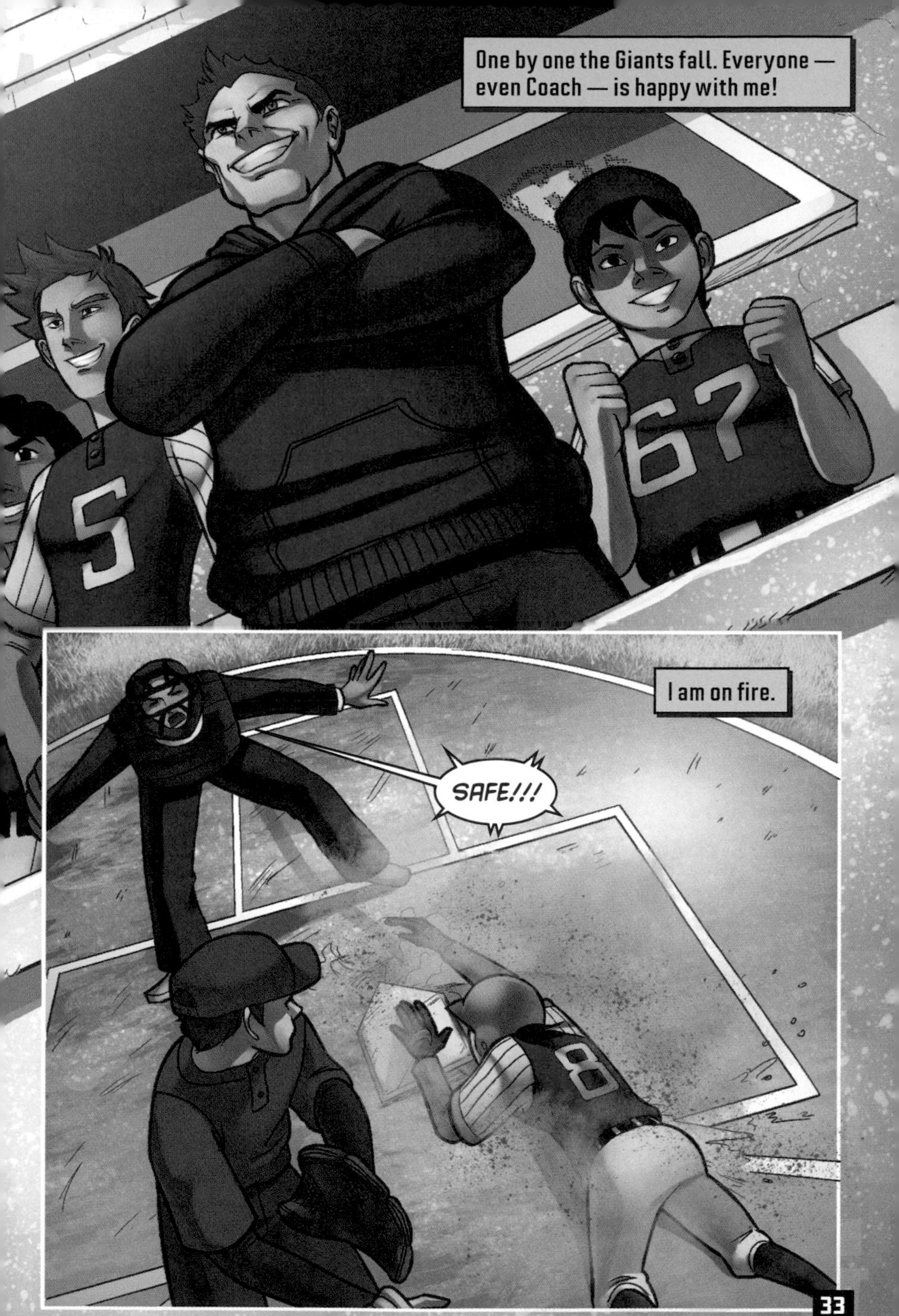
One by one the Giants fall. Everyone — even Coach — is happy with me!
I am on fire.
SAFE!!!

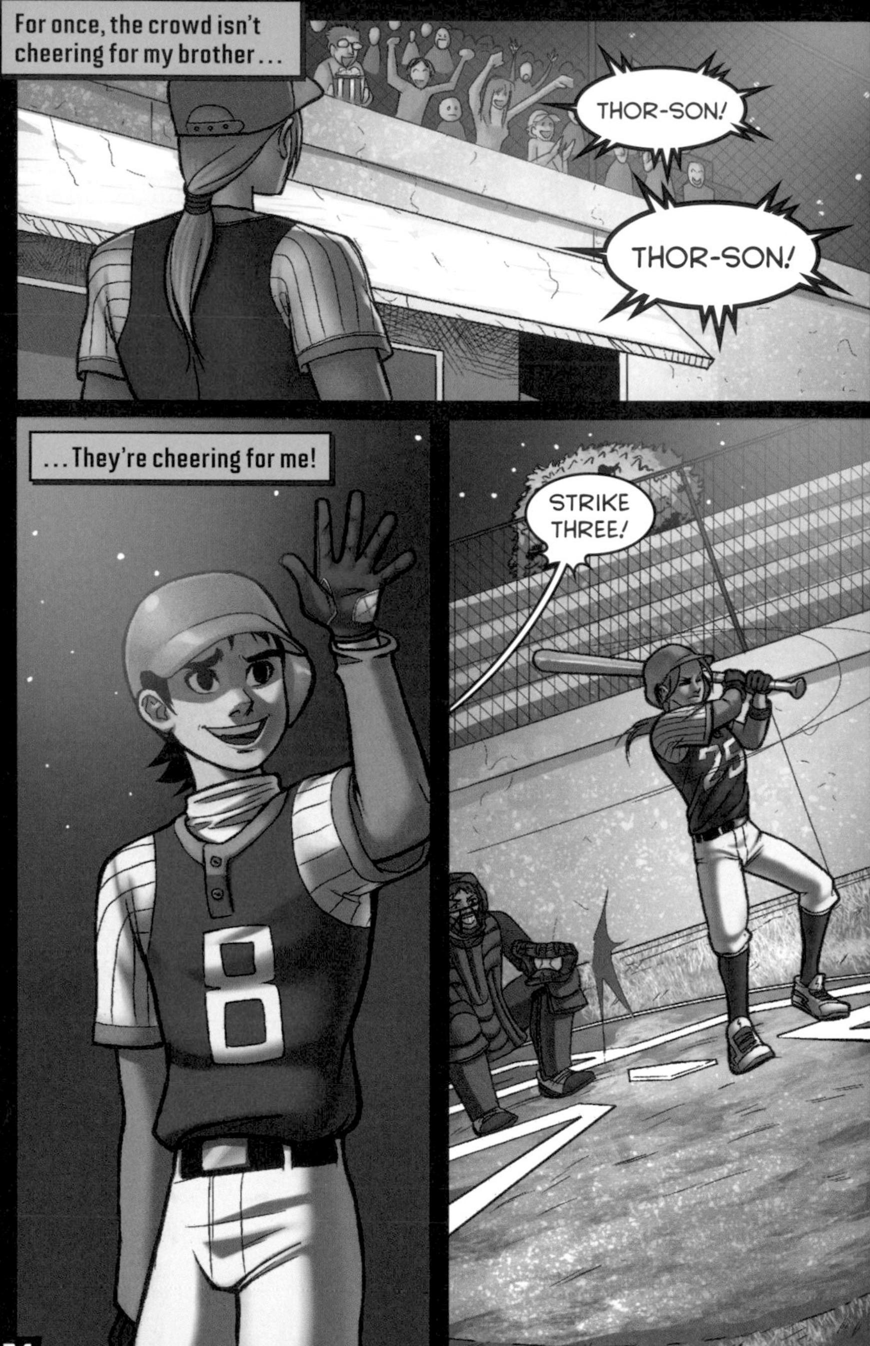
For once, the crowd isn't cheering for my brother . . .
THOR-SON!
THOR-SON!
. . . They're cheering for me!
STRIKE THREE!

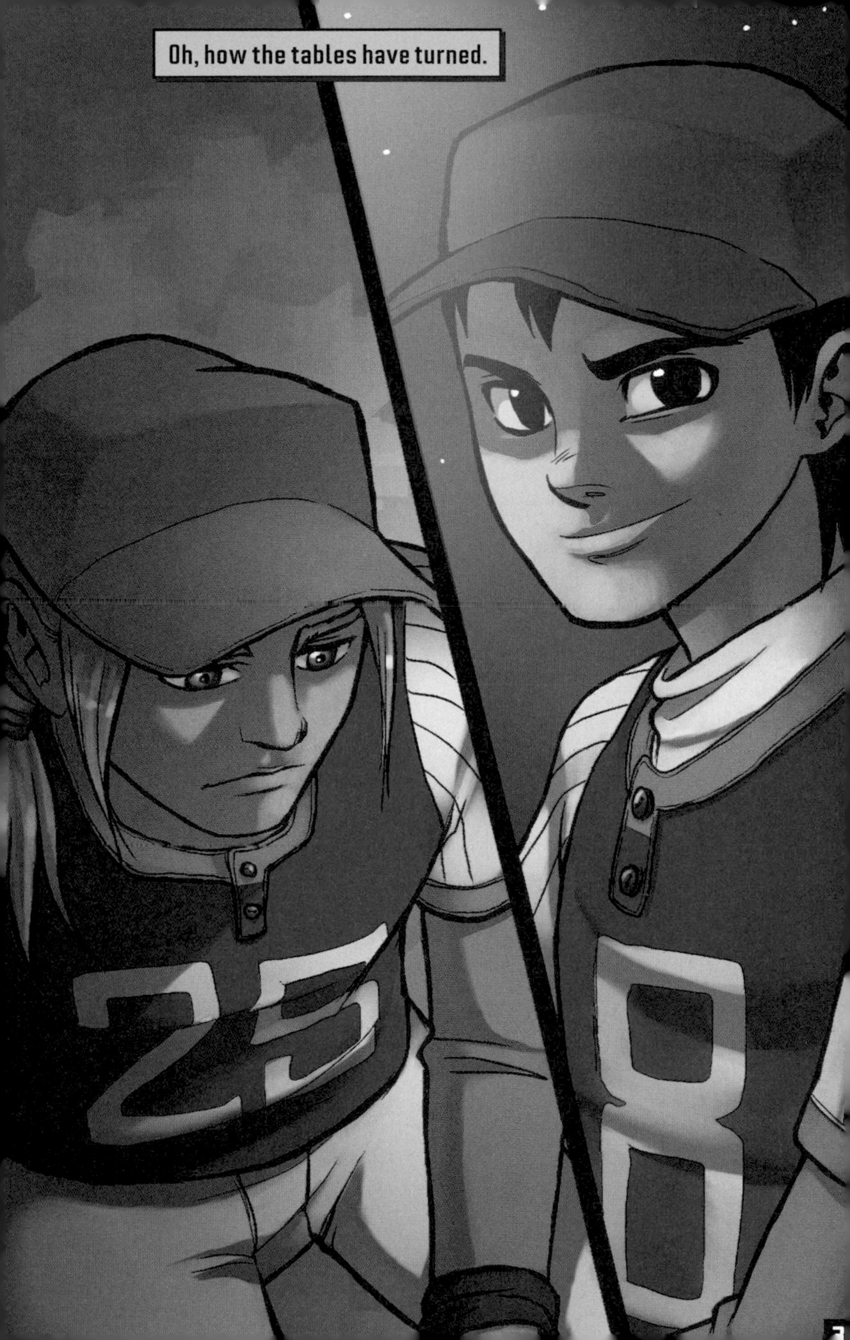
Oh, how the tables have turned.

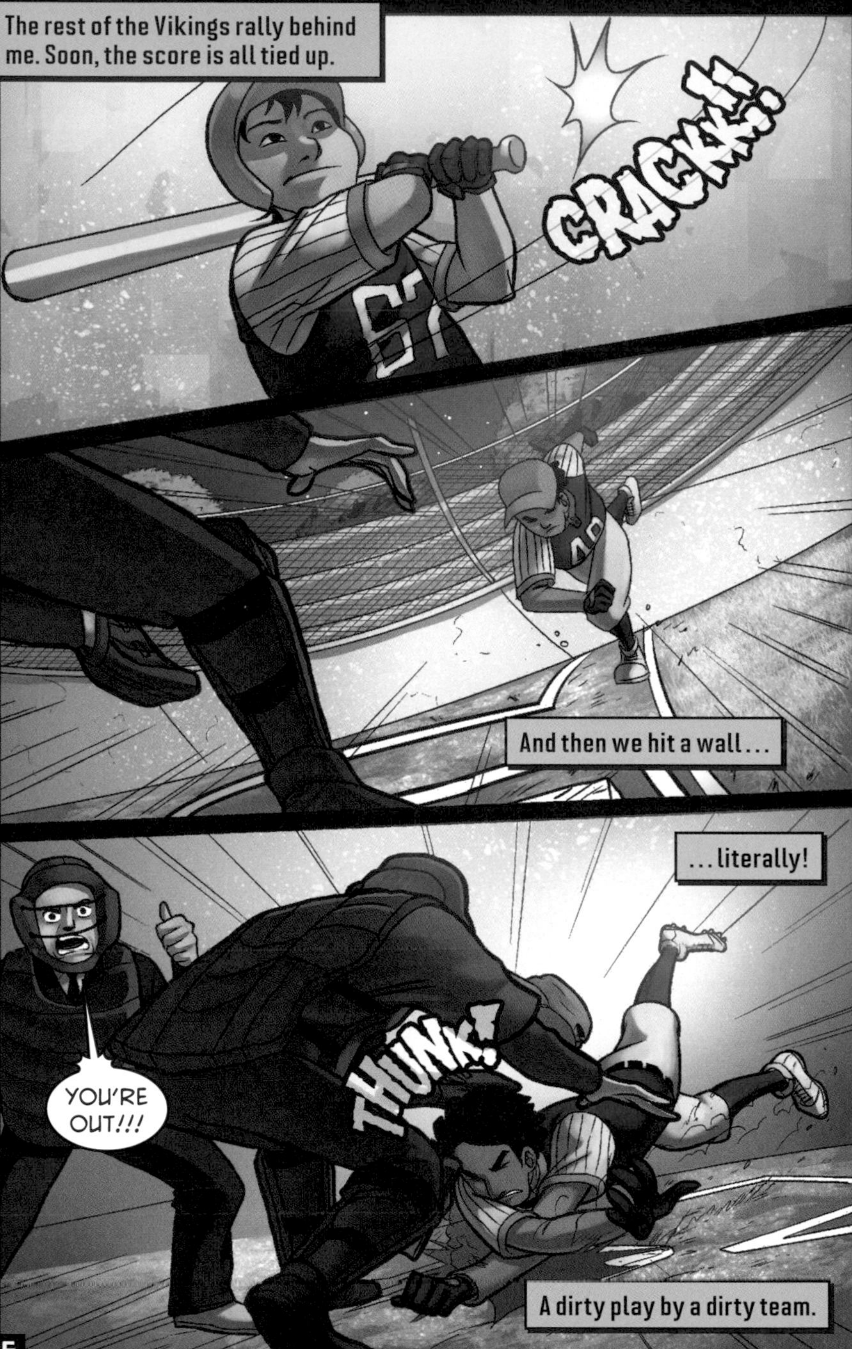
The rest of the Vikings rally behind me. Soon, the score is all tied up.
CRACK!!
And then we hit a wall . . .
. . . literally!
THUNK!
YOU'RE OUT!!!
A dirty play by a dirty team.

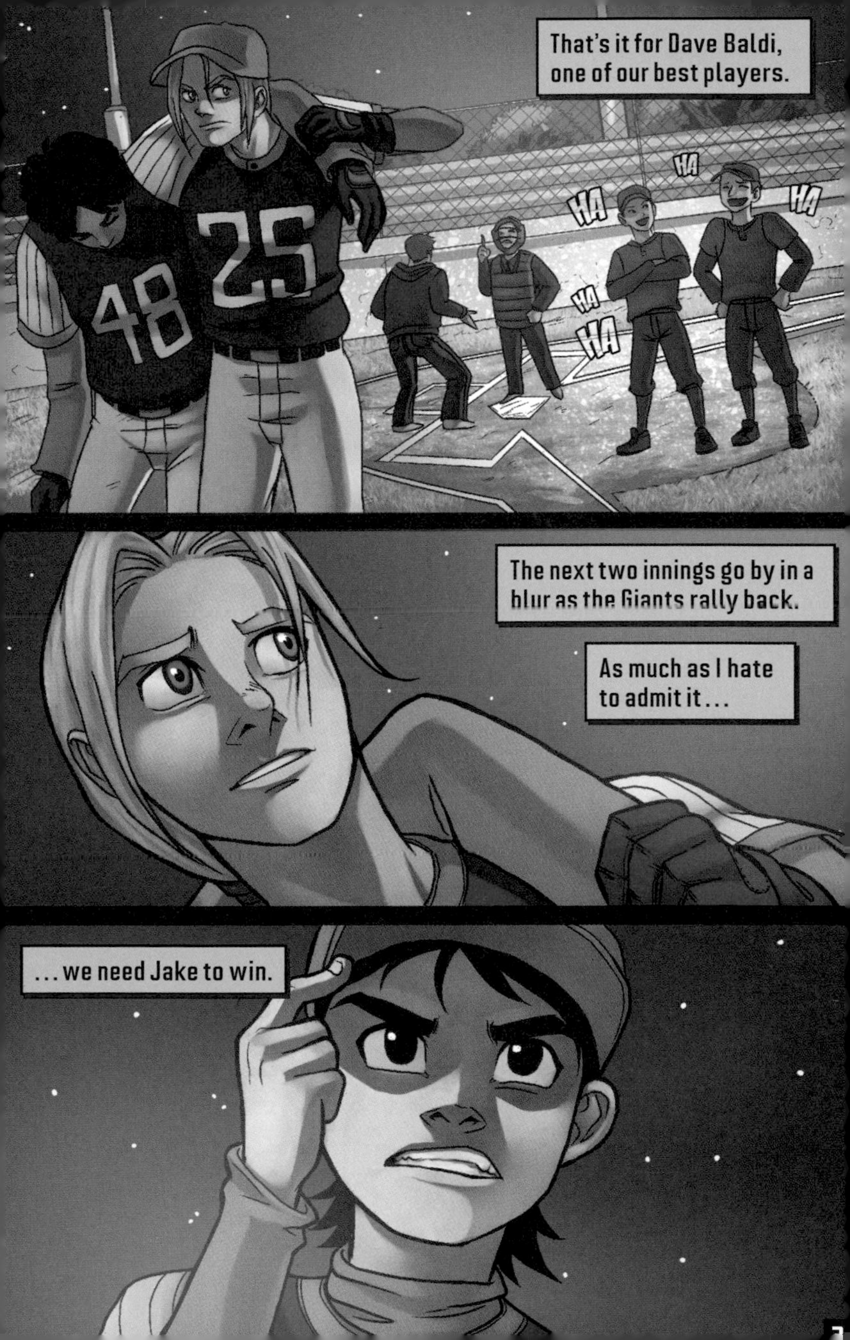
That's it for Dave Baldi, one of our best players.
HA
HA
HA
HA
HA
The next two innings go by in a blur as the Giants rally back.
As much as I hate to admit it . . .
. . . we need Jake to win.

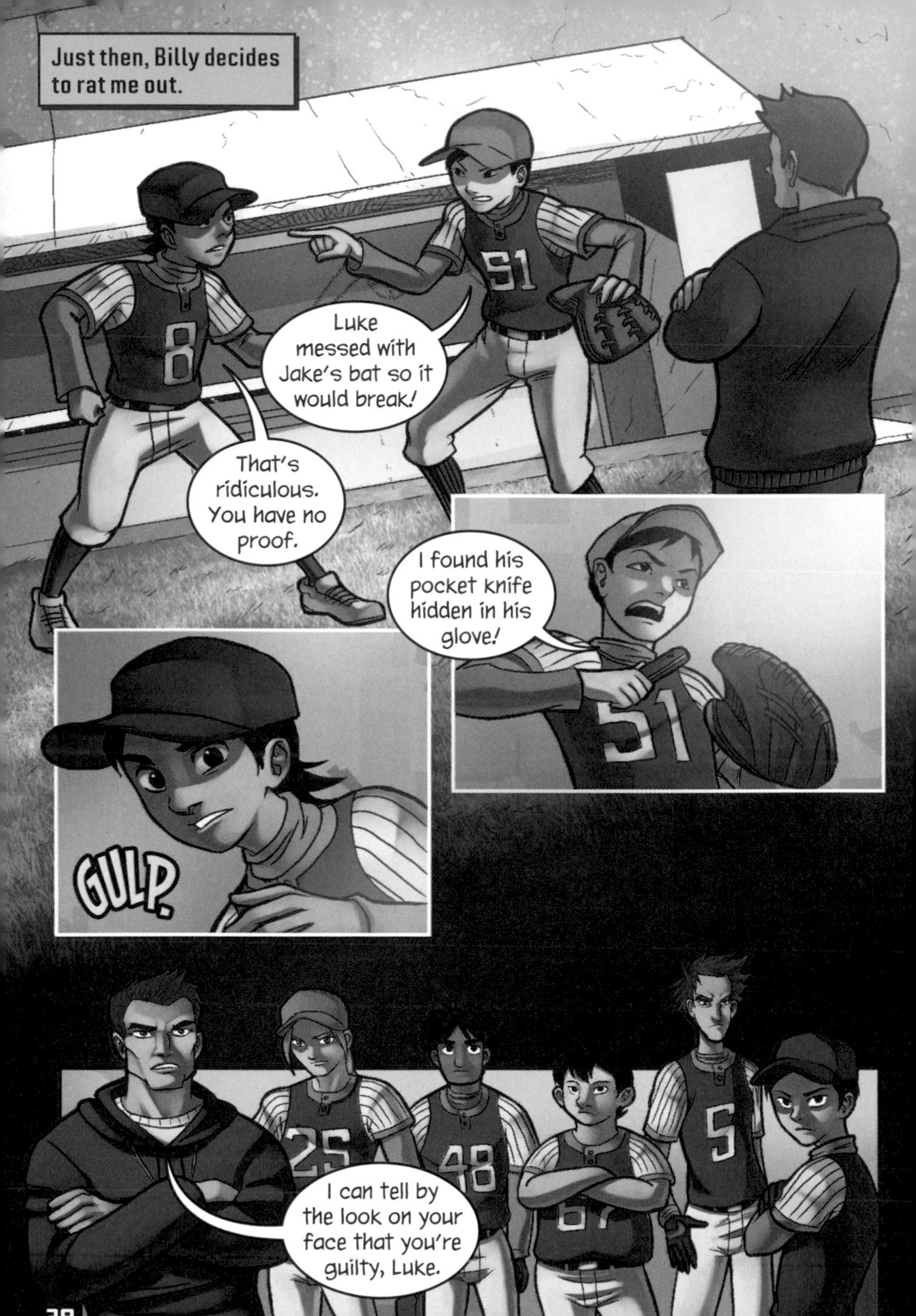
Just then, Billy decides to rat me out.
Luke messed with Jake's bat so it would break!
That's ridiculous. You have no proof.
I found his pocket knife hidden in his glove!
GULP.
I can tell by the look on your face that you're guilty, Luke.

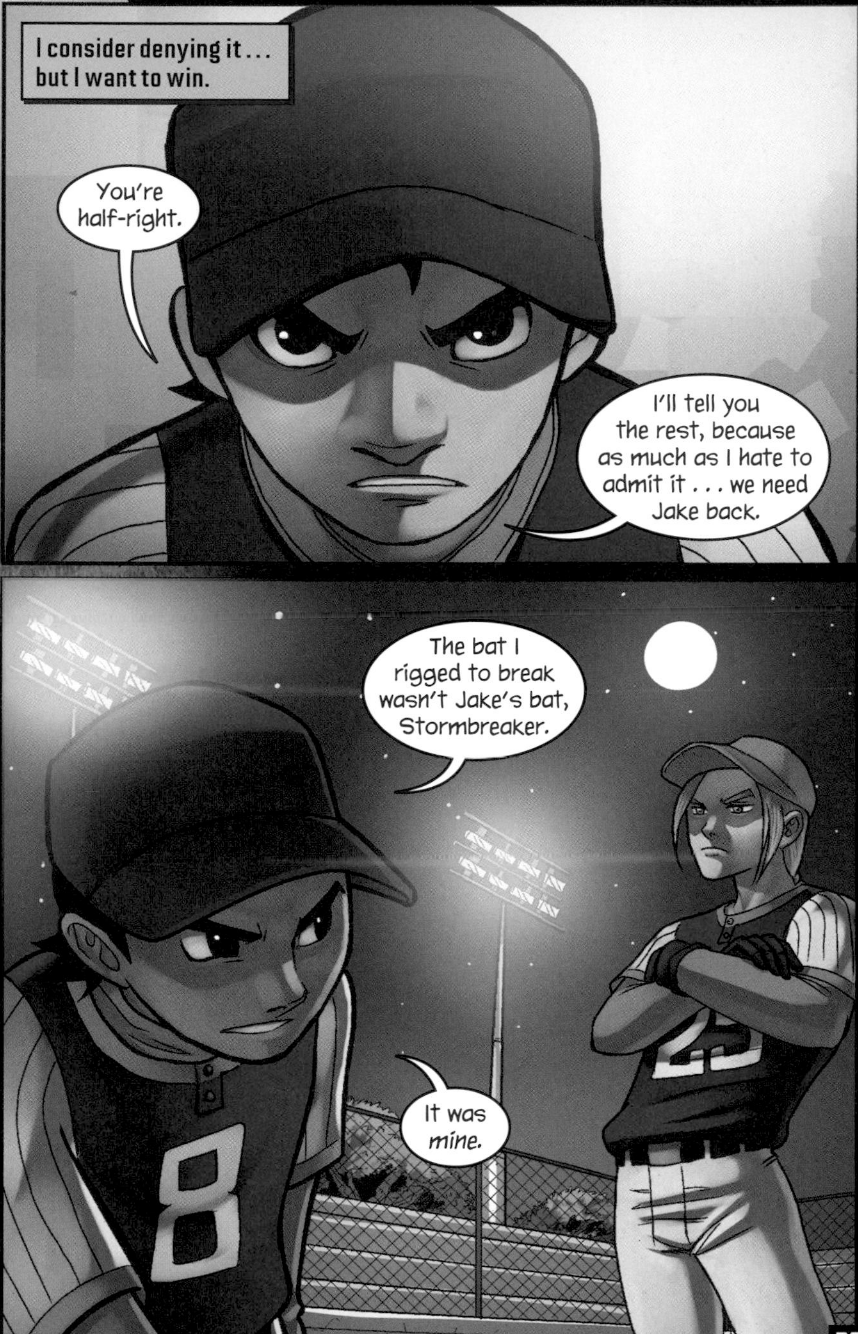
I consider denying it . . . but I want to win.
You're half-right.
I'll tell you the rest, because as much as I hate to admit it . . . we need Jake back.
The bat I rigged to break wasn't Jake's bat, Stormbreaker.
It was mine.

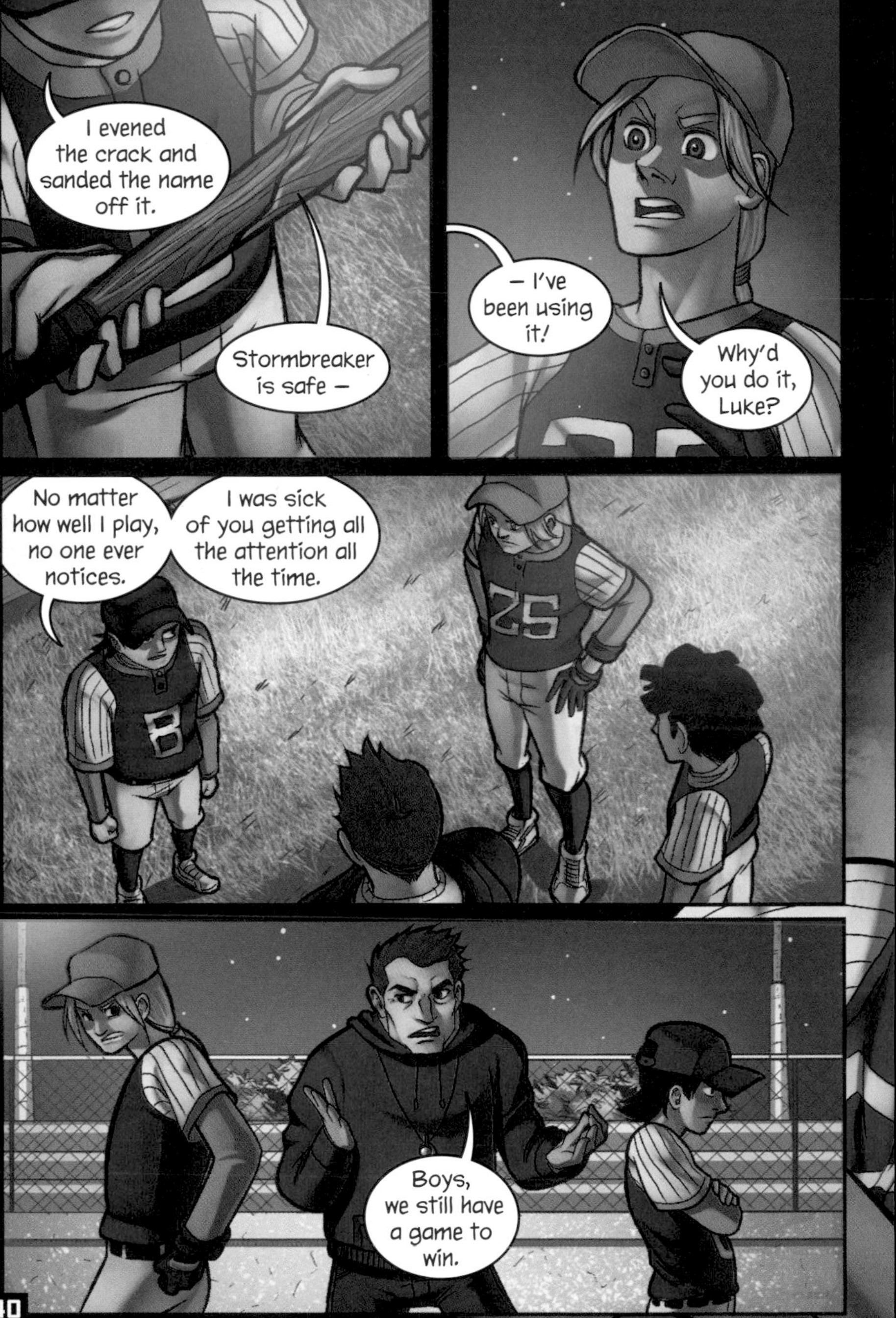
I evened the crack and sanded the name off it.
Stormbreaker is safe —
— I've been using it!
Why'd you do it, Luke?
No matter how well I play, no one ever notices.
I was sick of you getting all the attention all the time.
Boys, we still have a game to win.

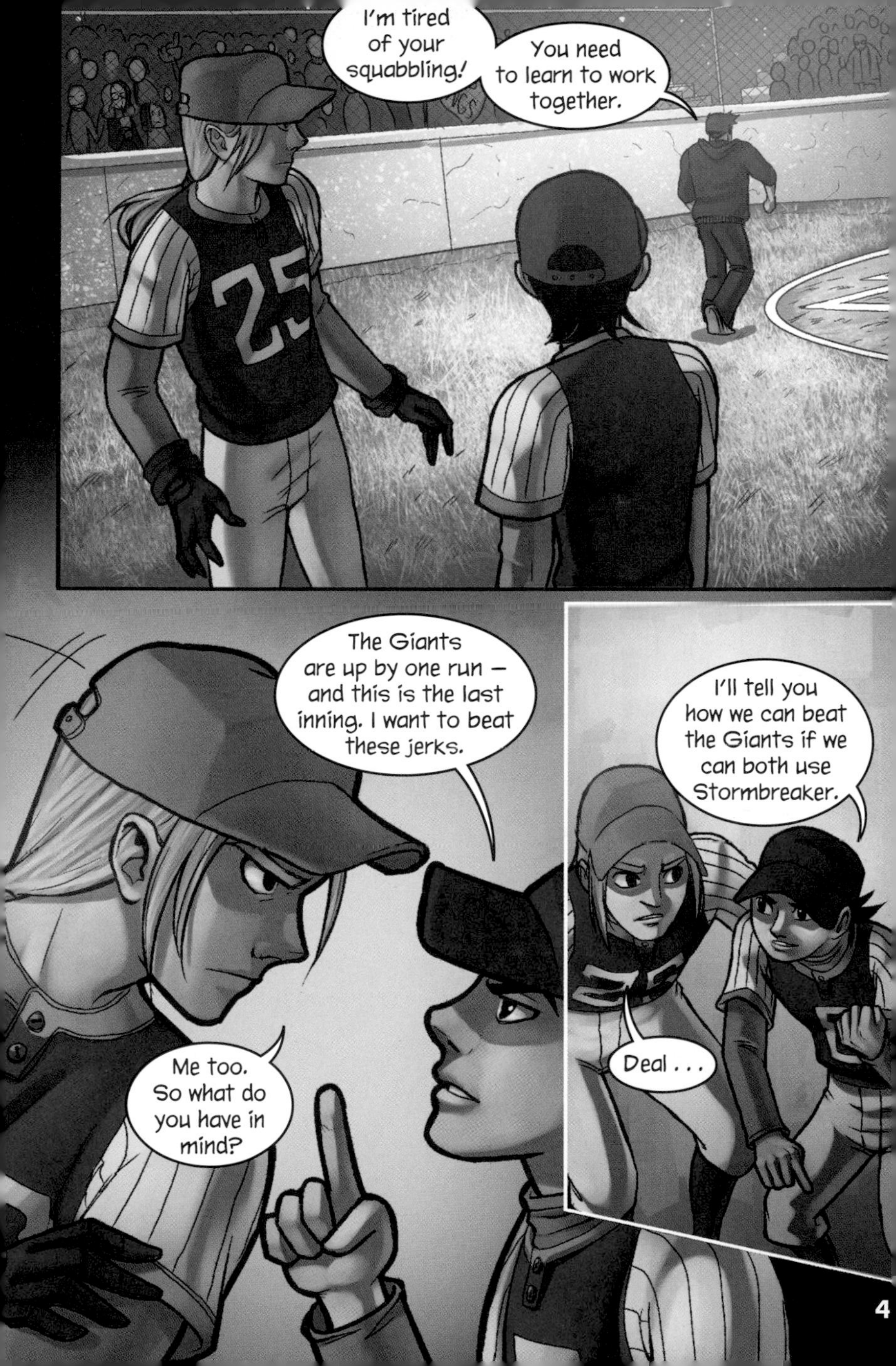
I'm tired of your squabbling!
You need to learn to work together.
The Giants are up by one run — and this is the last inning. I want to beat these jerks.
Me too. So what do you have in mind?
I'll tell you how we can beat the Giants if we can both use Stormbreaker.
Deal . . .

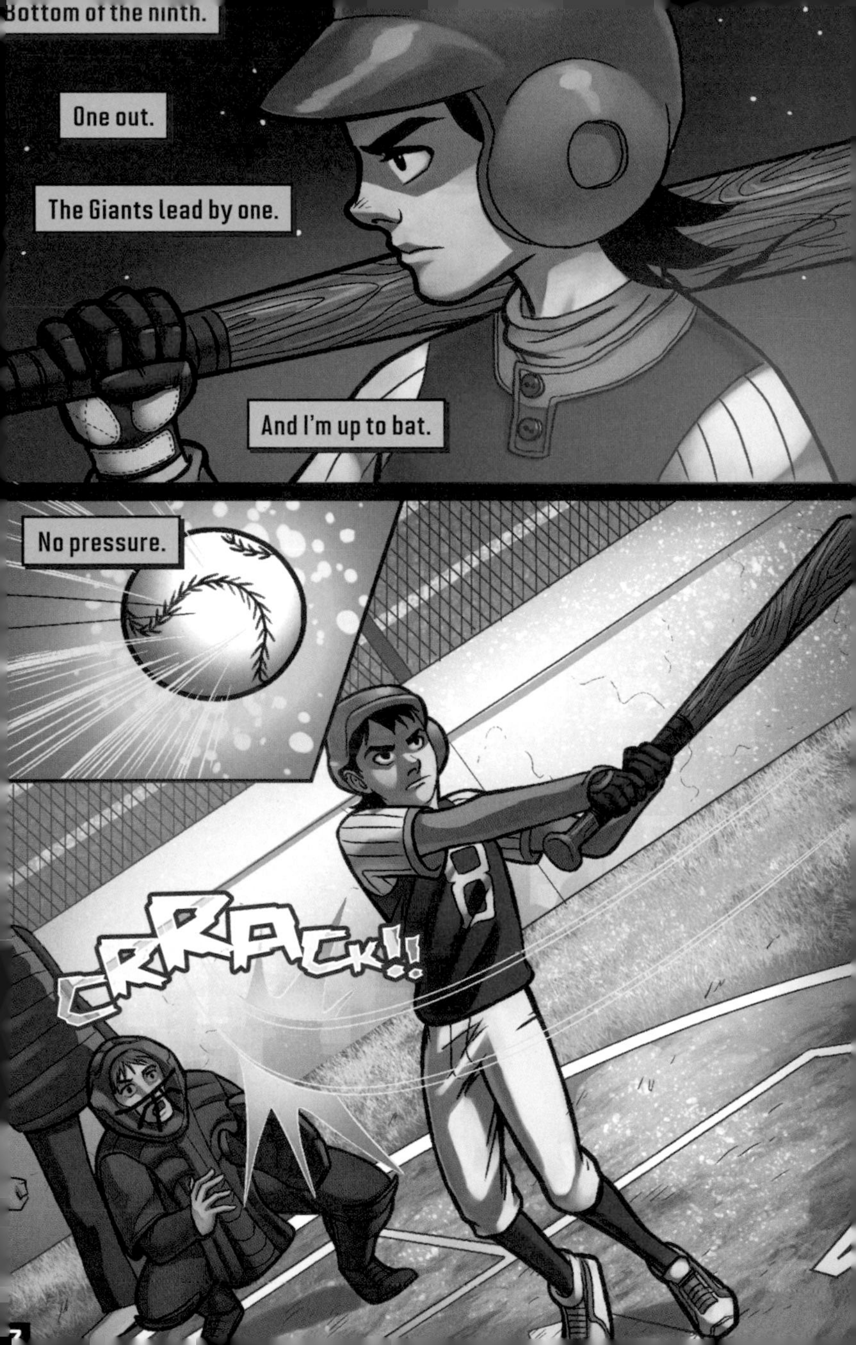
Bottom of the ninth.
One out.
The Giants lead by one.
And I'm up to bat.
No pressure.
CRRACK!!

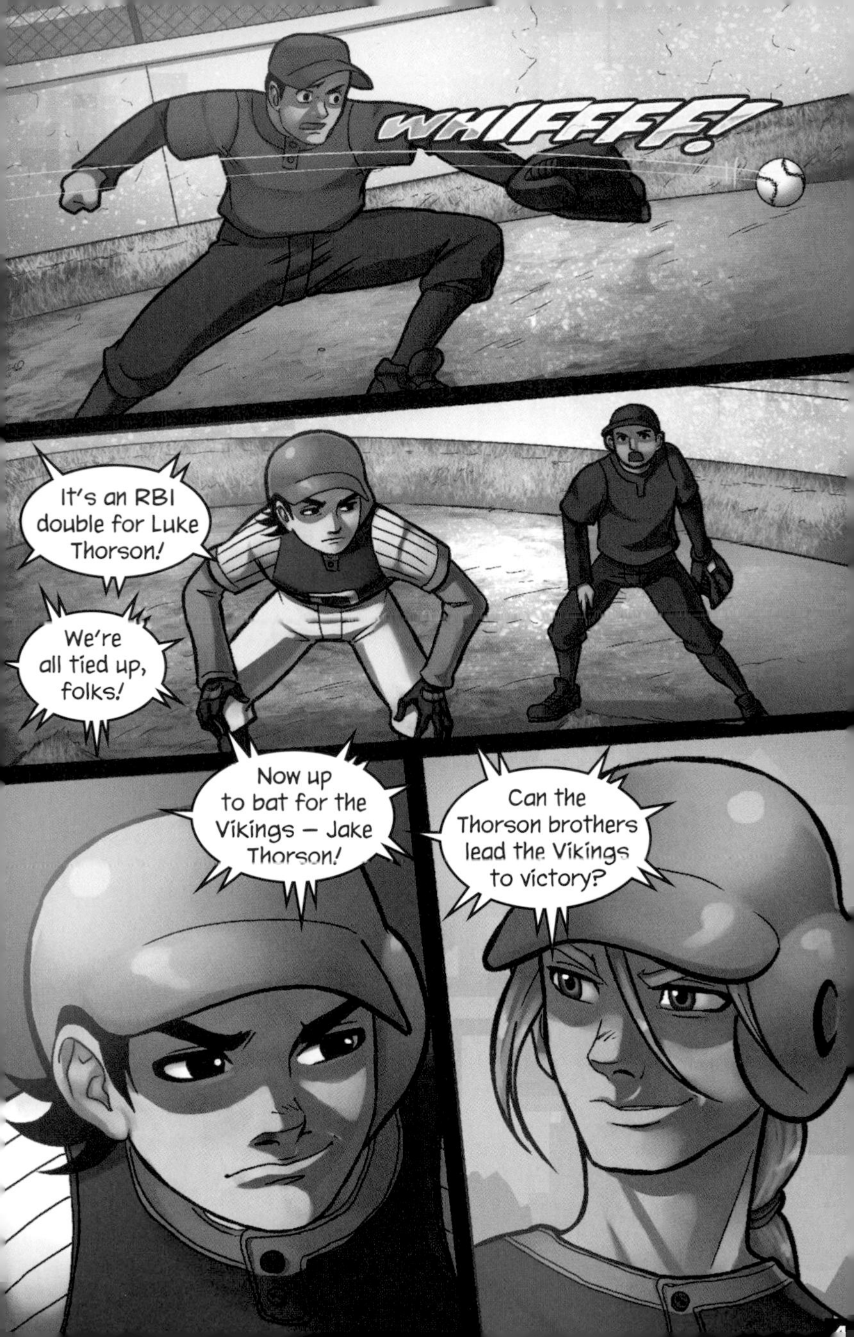
WHIFFFF!
It's an RBI double for Luke Thorson!
We're all tied up, folks!
Now up to bat for the Vikings — Jake Thorson!
Can the Thorson brothers lead the Vikings to victory?

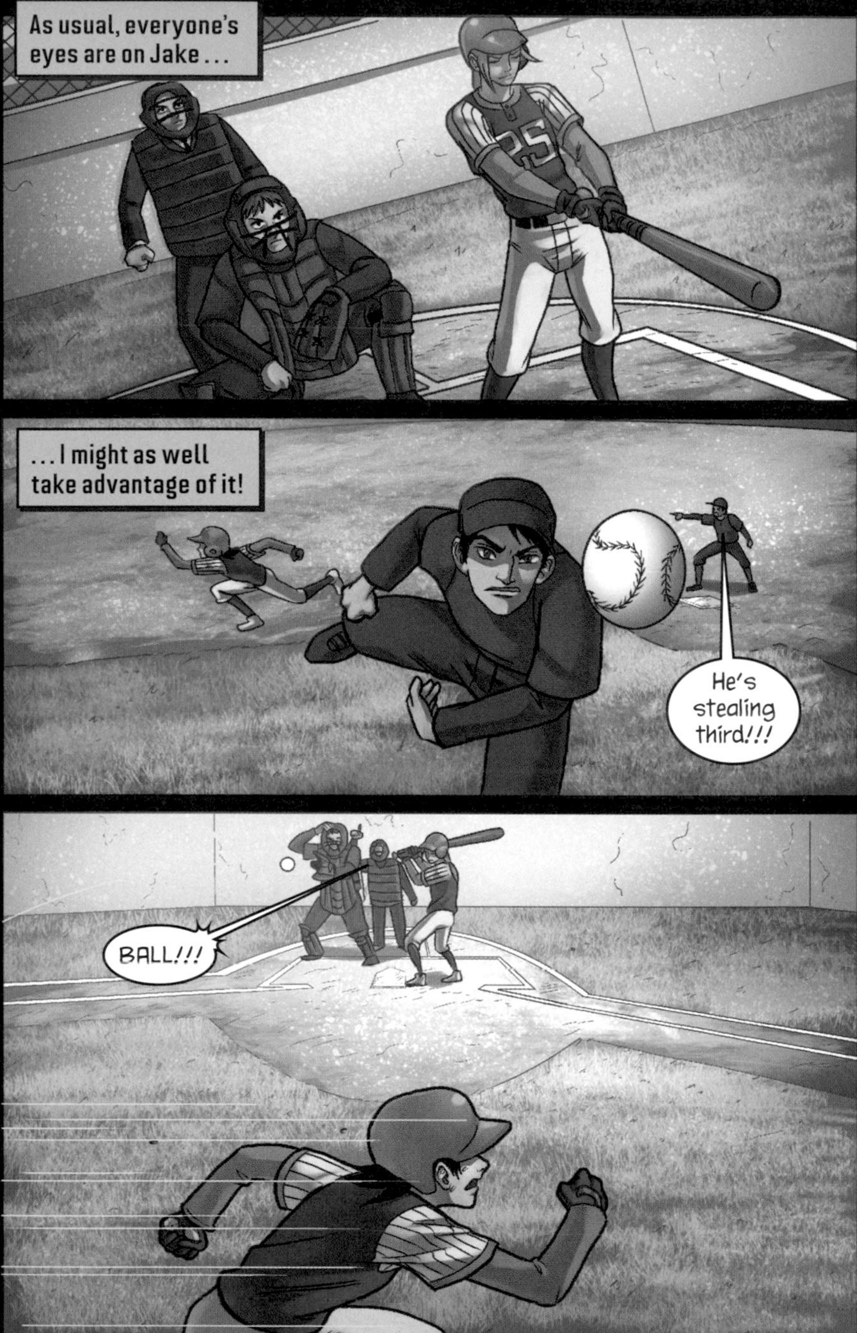

As usual, everyone's eyes are on Jake . . .
. . . I might as well take advantage of it!
He's stealing third!!!
BALL!!!

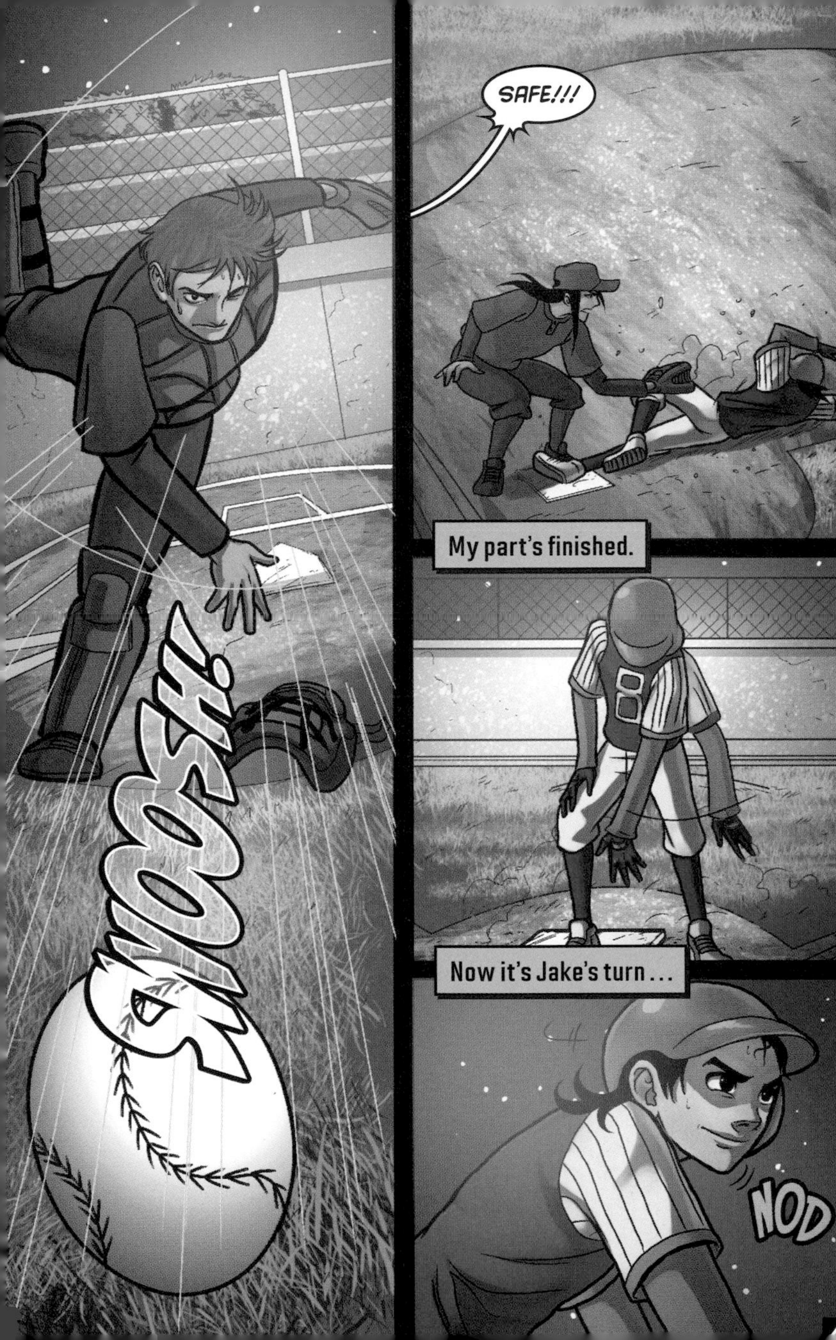
SWOOSH!!
SAFE!!!
My part's finished.
Now it's Jake's turn . . .
NOD

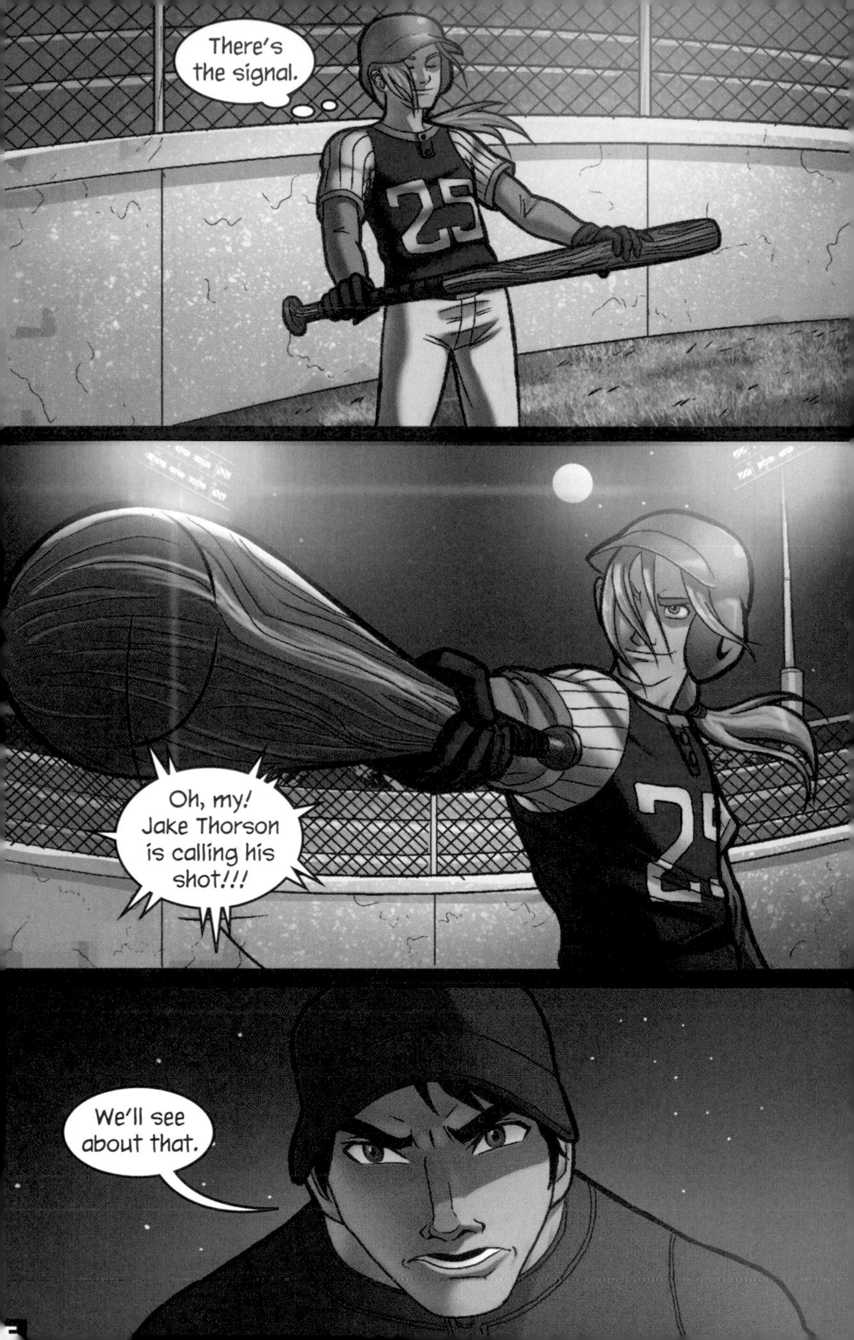
There's the signal.
Oh, my! Jake Thorson is calling his shot!!!
We'll see about that.

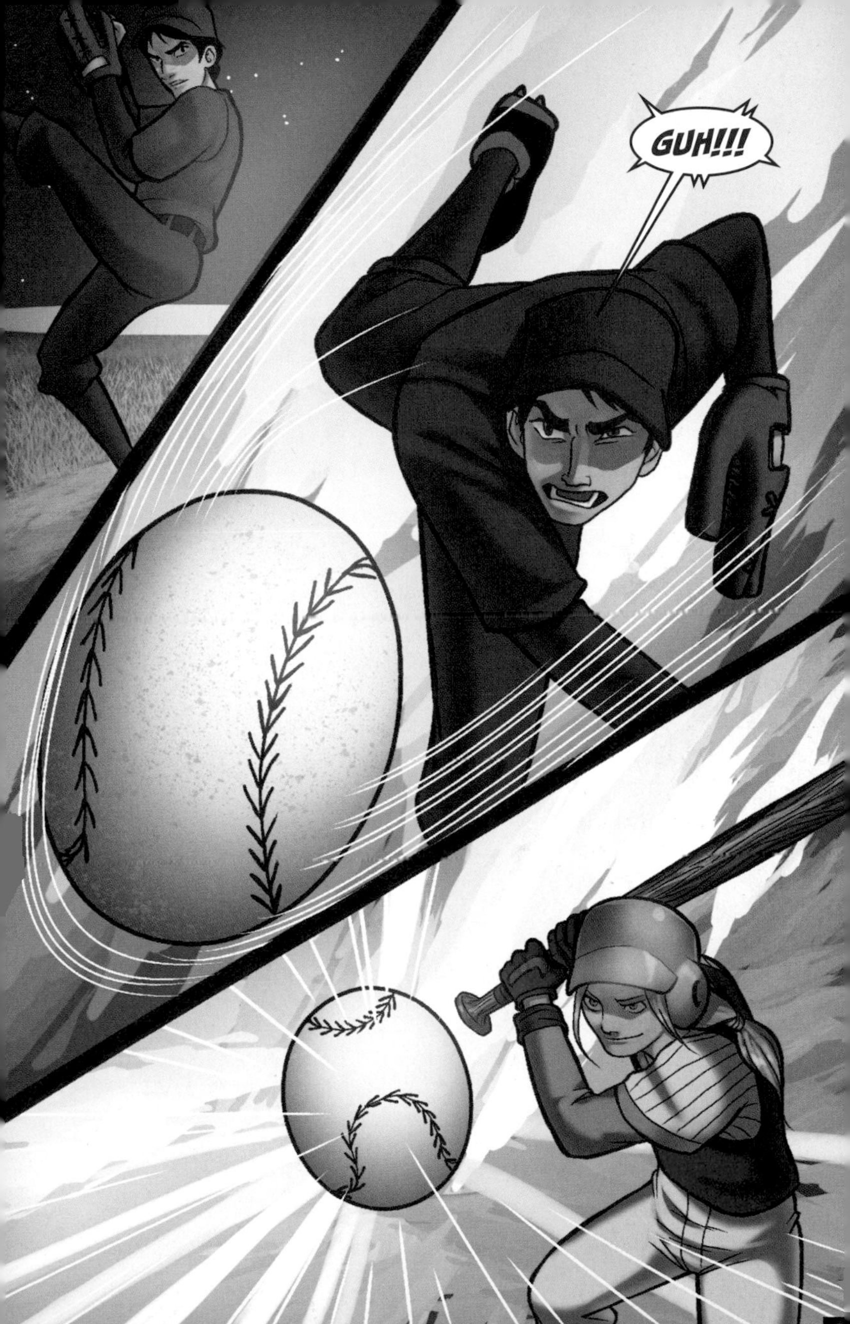
GUH!!!

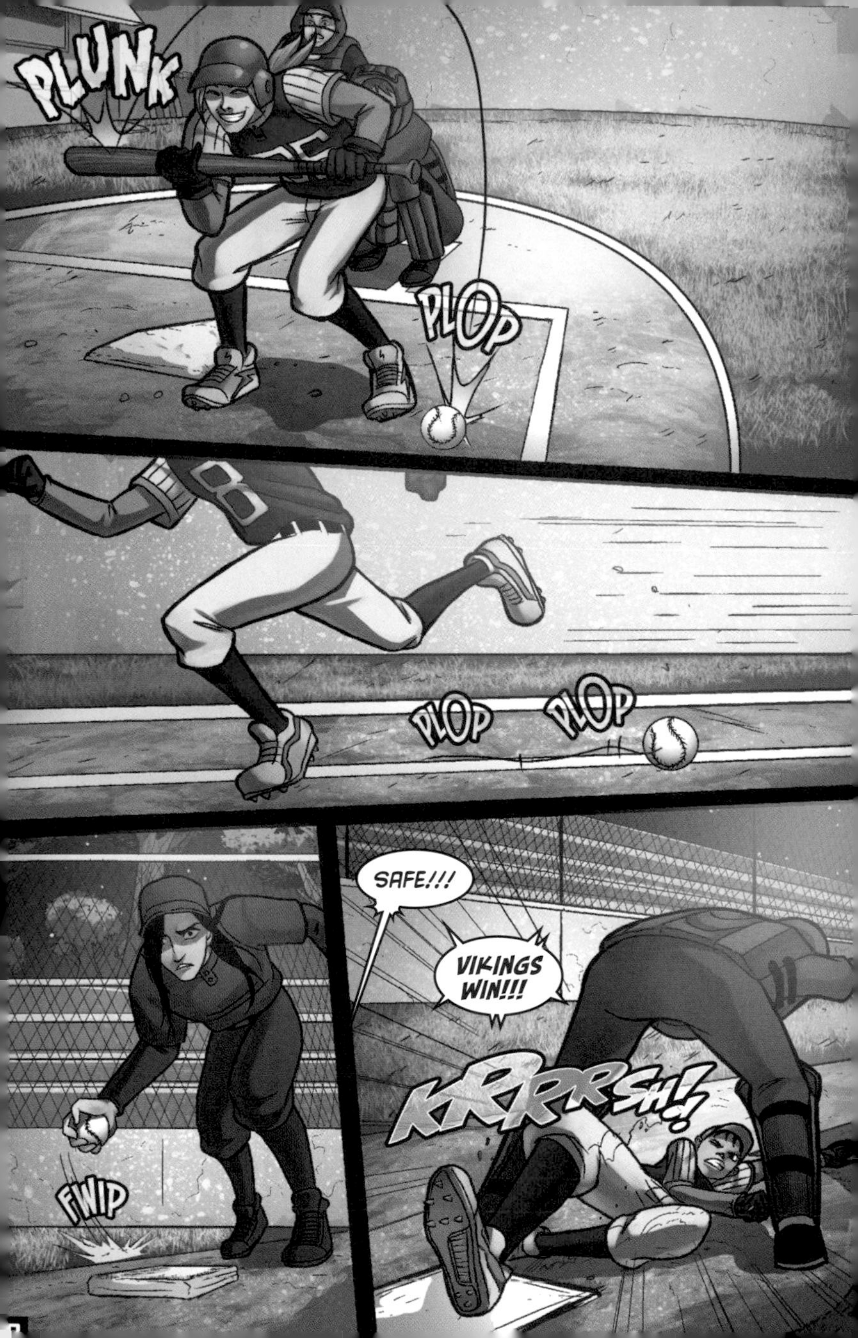
PLUNK
PLOP
PLOP
PLOP
FWIP
SAFE!!!
VIKINGS WIN!!!
KRRRSH!

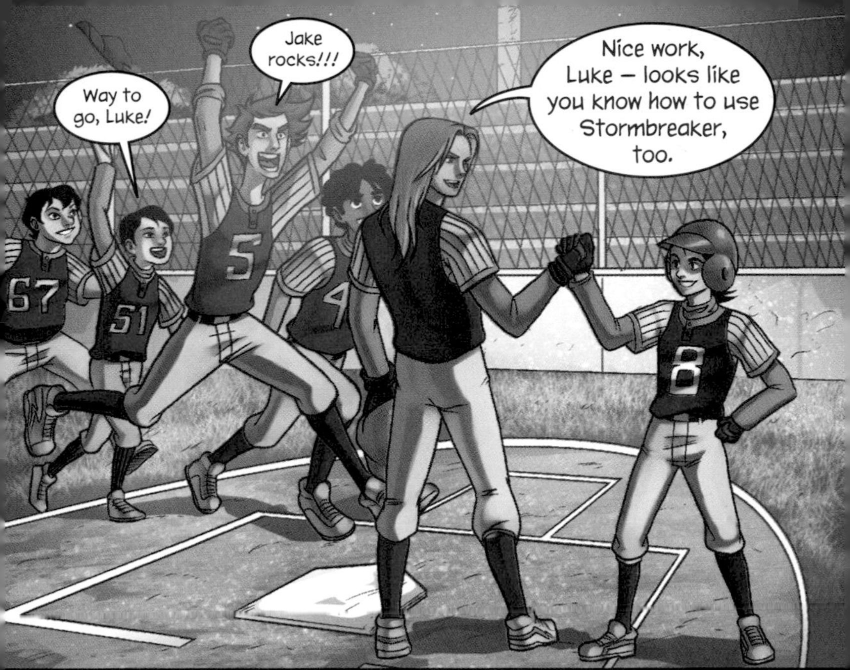
Way to go, Luke!
Jake rocks!!!
Nice work, Luke – looks like you know how to use Stormbreaker, too.

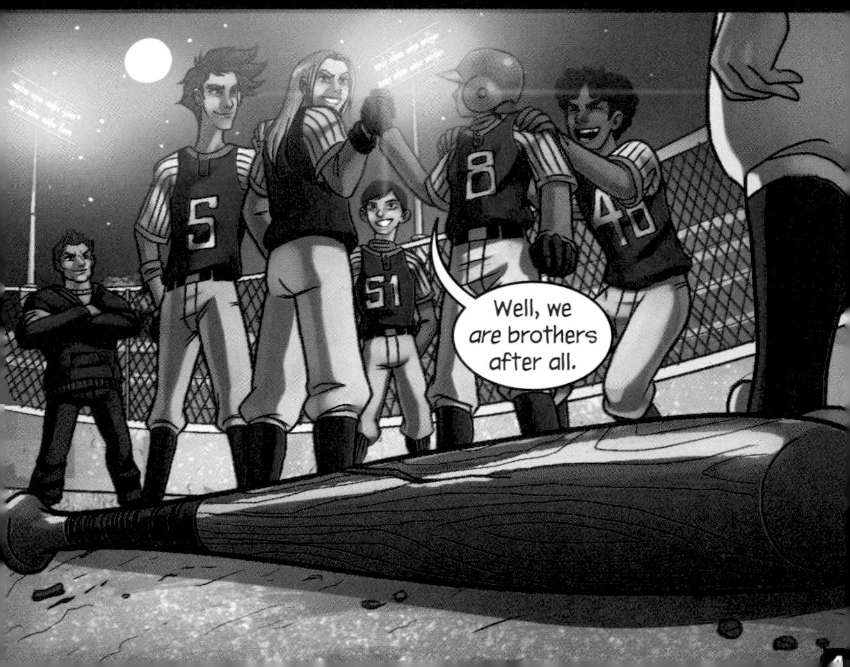
Well, we *are* brothers after all.

SPORTS ZONE
POSTGAME RECAP

BSL
BASEBALL

PNT
PAINTBALL

SOC
SOCCER

FBL
FOOTBALL

BBL
BASKETBALL

HKY

THORSON BROTHERS TEAM UP TO TOPPLE THE GIANTS!

BY THE NUMBERS

STATS LEADERS:
HITS: LUKE, 3
STRIKEOUTS: DAVIS, 5
HOMERUNS: JAKE, 1

STORY: Rumors of bat-related sabotage swirled today as stepbrothers Luke and Jake Thorson argued on the field. But whatever problems these two teens had vanished when the game was on the line. With careful planning and solid skills, Luke and Jake set up the perfect scheme to beat the Giants into submission.

Sports Illustrated KIDS

UP NEXT: SI KIDS INFO CENTER

BLZ vs BHS 3-1
TGR vs RDR 33-32
EAG vs BAN 14-7
SPA vs WLD 4-3
BAN vs RDR 21-15
RZR vs LIG 4-3
BLZ vs BHS 3-1

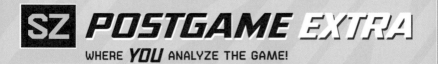

SZ POSTGAME EXTRA

WHERE ***YOU*** ANALYZE THE GAME!

Baseball fans got a real treat today when the Vikings took out the Giants in a competitive baseball battle. Let's go into the stands and ask some fans for their opinions on the day's big game . . .

DISCUSSION QUESTION 1

Jake and Luke are stepbrothers. Do you have any siblings or step-siblings? What kinds of things do you and your family members argue about?

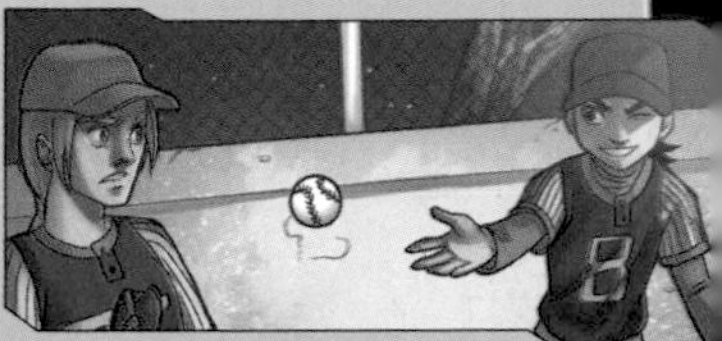

DISCUSSION QUESTION 2

Which Viking did you like more — Jake or Luke? Why?

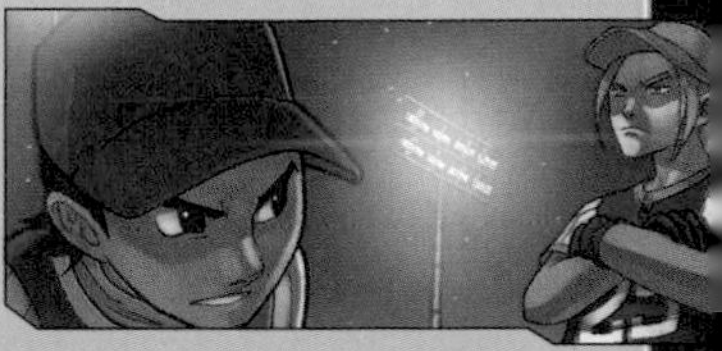

WRITING PROMPT 1

Jake's bat is nicknamed "Stormbreaker." Give yourself a nickname and write about why you chose it and how it fits you.

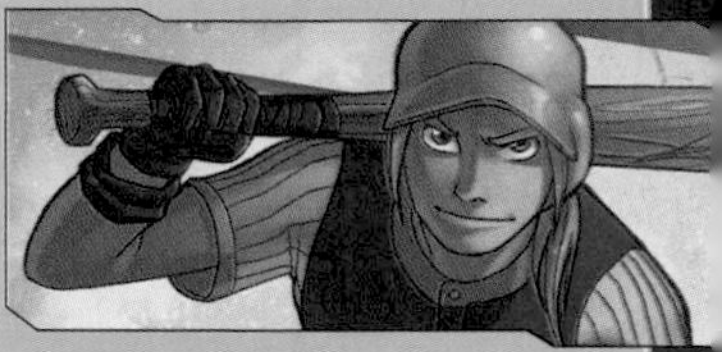

WRITING PROMPT 2

What is your favorite position in baseball? What's your favorite pitch? Favorite team? Write about all your baseball favorites.

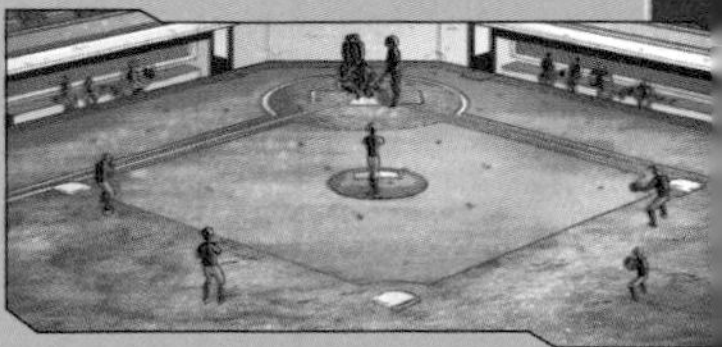

Sports Illustrated KIDS

INFO CENTER

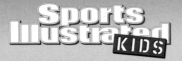

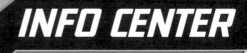

GLOSSARY

CONFIDENT (KON-fuh-duhnt)—having strong belief in your abilities, or that something will happen in the way you want

PAYBACK (PAY-bak)—revenge

RALLIED (RAL-eed)—brought together, united, or teamed up

RBI (R-B-I)—RBIs, also known as runs batted in, are statistics given to a batter when a hit causes a runner to score

REPUTATION (rep-yoo-TAY-shuhn)—your reputation is what other people think or say about you

RIDICULOUS (ri-DIK-yuh-luhss)—extremely silly or foolish

SIGNAL (SIG-nuhl)—anything agreed upon to send a message or warning, like a hand sign in baseball

CREATORS

Scott Ciencin › Author

Scott Ciencin is a *New York Times* bestselling author of children's and adult fiction. He has written comic books, trading cards, video games, television shows, as well as many non-fiction projects. He lives in Sarasota, Florida with his beloved wife, Denise, and his best buddy, Bear, a golden retriever.

Zoar Huerta › Penciler

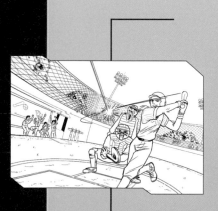

Zoar Huerta (also known as "Charecua") studied Communication at Universidad Veracruzana. She currently works as a penciler and illustrator for Graphikslava. She works for some local magazines in her spare time, and she's a rookie penciler in the comic book industry. Zoar is always looking for more illustration work in order to pay for her expensive and exotic lifestyle.

Angelica Bracho › Inker

Angelica Bracho was born in Monterrey, Mexico, where she later studied Visual Arts. Today, she's part of the Graphikslava illustration team. Her work has been published in magazines, and she has illustrated some IDW Publishing titles. She loves to present her illustration work at alternative Mexican art galleries.

Fernando Cano › Colorist

Fernando Cano is an emerging illustrator born in Mexico City, Mexico. He currently resides in Monterrey, Mexico, where he works as a full-time illustrator and colorist at Graphikslava studio. He has done illustration work for Marvel, DC Comics, and role-playing games like Pathfinder from Paizo Publishing. In his spare time, he enjoys hanging out with friends, singing, rowing, and drawing!

Sports Illustrated KIDS
GRAPHIC NOVELS
QUICK COMIC

KYLE WALKER and RYAN ROGAN IN:
WILD PITCH

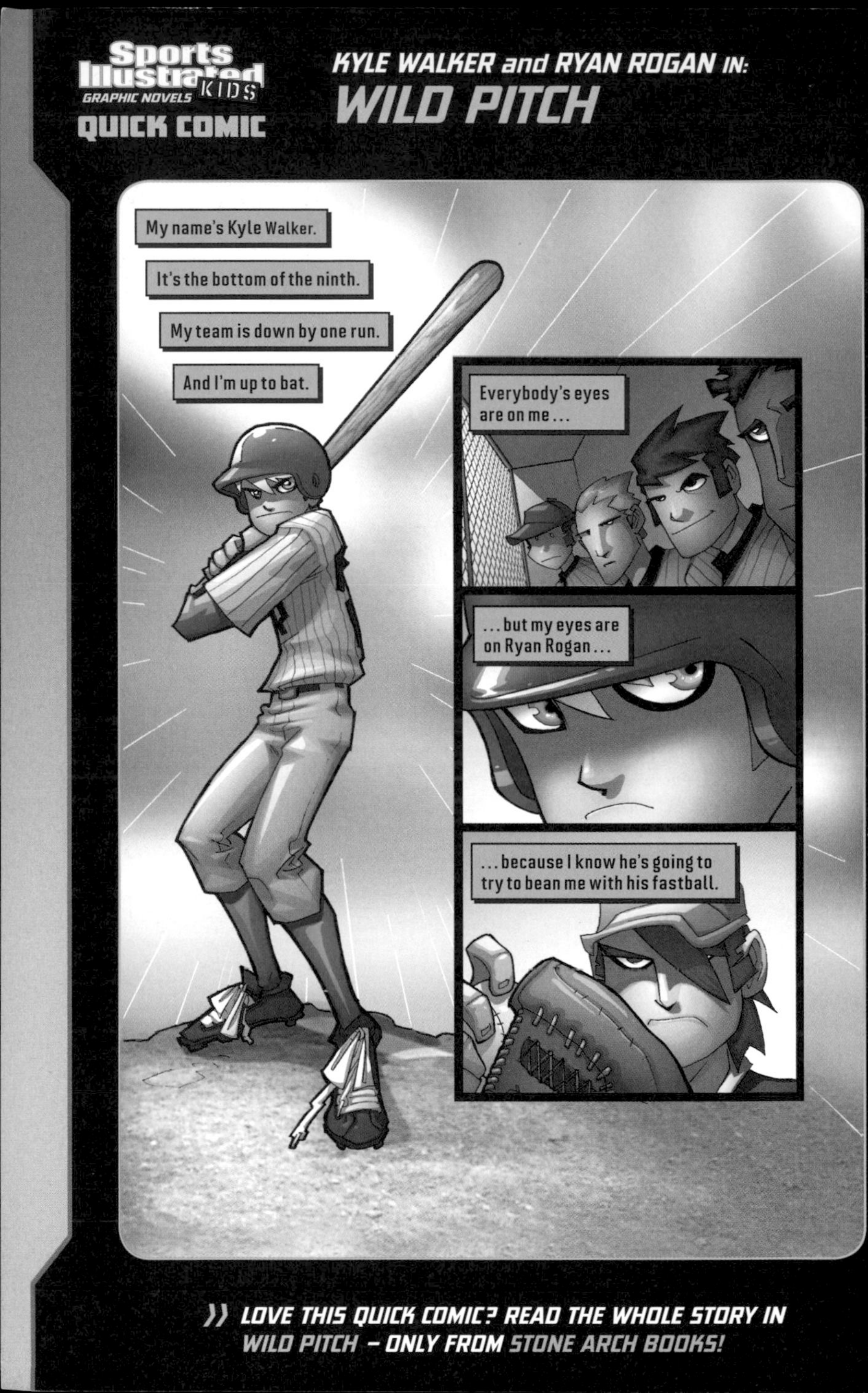

My name's Kyle Walker.
It's the bottom of the ninth.
My team is down by one run.
And I'm up to bat.
Everybody's eyes are on me . . .
. . . but my eyes are on Ryan Rogan . . .
. . . because I know he's going to try to bean me with his fastball.

)) LOVE THIS QUICK COMIC? READ THE WHOLE STORY IN WILD PITCH – ONLY FROM STONE ARCH BOOKS!

HOT SPORTS. HOT FORMAT!

GREAT CHARACTERS BATTLE FOR SPORTS GLORY IN TODAY'S HOTTEST FORMAT—GRAPHIC NOVELS!

ONLY FROM STONE ARCH BOOKS

Sports Illustrated KIDS
GRAPHIC NOVELS

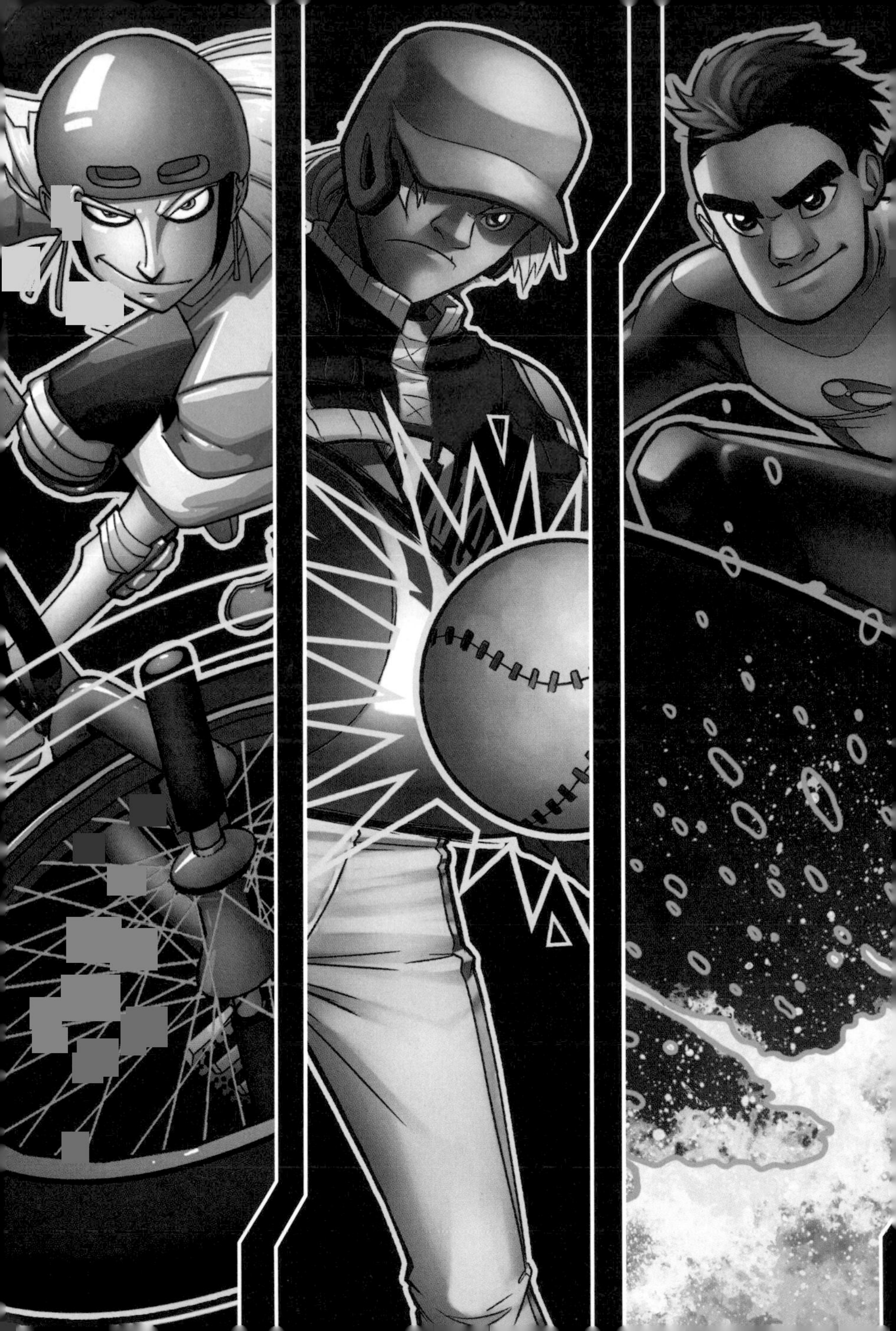